Praise for J. L. Bourne's Day by Day Armageddon

"There is zombie fiction and then there is crawl-out-of-the-grave-and-drag-you-to-hell zombie fiction. *Day by Day Armageddon* is hands-down the best zombie book I have ever read. *Dawn of the Dead* meets *28 Days Later* doesn't even come close to describing how fantastic this thriller is. It is so real, so terrifying, and so well written that I slept with not one, but two loaded Glocks under my pillow for weeks afterwards. J. L. Bourne is the new king of hardcore zombie action!"

—Brad Thor, #1 *New York Times* bestselling author of *The Last Patriot* and *The First Commandment*

"*Day by Day Armageddon* is a dramatic spin on the zombie story. It has depth, a heart, and compelling characters."

—Jonathan Maberry, Bram Stoker Award–winning author of *Ghost Road Blues*

"*Day by Day Armageddon* claws at the reader's mind. Bourne's journal is a visceral insight into the psyche of a skilled survivor."

—Gregory Solis, author of *Rise and Walk*

Day by Day Armageddon

by

J. L. Bourne

Introduction by Z.A. RECHT

POCKET BOOKS
New York London Toronto Sydney

Pocket Books
A Division of Simon & Schuster, Inc.
1230 Avenue of the Americas
New York, NY 10020

Originally published in 2007 by Permuted Press

First Pocket Books trade paperback edition September 2009

Editing and interior design by Travis Adkins

Manufactured in the United States of America

10 9 8 7 6 5 4 3 2 1

Library of Congress Cataloging-in-Publication Data is available

ISBN 978-1-4391-7667-2
ISBN 978-1-4391-7727-3 (ebook)

For more information about Permuted Press books and authors, visit www.permutedpress.com.

Introduction

by Z. A. Recht

I've been a zombie fan for years. I can safely say that I've spent more than half my life as a hopeless addict to anything and everything undead. I'd go out and buy a book or a movie just because it used the word *zombie* somewhere in the title. Needless to say, this method of shopping left me with some horrible disappointments ("Night of the Zombies") and some french-fried gold ("Redneck Zombies").

Most of these were the result of pure happenstance. I'd be out looking for one thing, and stumble onto my beloved genre. Nothing can sidetrack me like zombies—so, with that established, you'll understand why, several years ago, I vanished off of the face of the planet for one full day. Phone calls went unanswered. E-mails went unresponded to. I'm pretty sure I forgot to eat. I know I didn't forget to chainsmoke. I never forget to chainsmoke.

Anyway, the reason behind this sudden withdrawal into my own little universe was the discovery of this amazing online chronicle of one man trying to stay alive in a world overrun by the undead—and get this: it wasn't just some fanfic. It covered the main character's journey *day* by *day* by agonizing *day*, from the very start of the undead infestation all the way through to one of the most nail-biting cliffhangers I've ever come to. I am, naturally, talking about *Day by Day Armageddon.*

I forget where I stumbled onto the link that led me to J.L. Bourne's chronicle of the zombie apocalypse, but I distinctly remember spending the next seven or eight hours reading from the very beginning all the way through to his most recent post. I'm a faster reader than that, but I was so into the story I'd stop every now and again to go over to the forum and see what other people had been saying about the entry I was on. I took that story and twisted it like a wet towel to get every last little drop of exposition I could out of it, and when I finally reached the end, it was too late—I was hooked. I am sure that there are crackheads out there who have similar stories about how they first got started. I had discovered the well-kept secret of zombie fiction on the internet thanks to *Day by Day Armageddon*. My first step was to register on Mr. Bourne's forum and start chatting it up with fellow zombie fans.

I should point out that up until that point my penchant for the undead was something that my friends in real life merely *tolerated*; suddenly, I was surrounded by people who actually *encouraged* it. They talked about the things I always liked to think about but never had anyone to discuss with: what gear would be best in the event of a zombie apocalypse, long-term survival planning, and always, always, *always* being prepared for the unexpected. All of which is, of course, sound advice no matter who you are, zombie fan or no.

So I bounced from forum to forum. I even dared to stick my head into a couple of politics threads, which is somewhat similar to shoving your hand into a pile of red-hot coals—You know it's going to burn, and you know it was a stupid thing to do in the first place, and for the life of you, you can't figure out why you did it. I needn't have worried; I was like a coin circling one of those donation funnels. I just had to give it a little more time and sooner or later I'd end up where I was supposed to be. That turned out to be the fiction board. Here were dozens of other stories of life in an undead world. I delved into them and tore through them. Funny thing about zombie fiction—unlike food, the more you consume, the hungrier you get. Pretty soon I decided I couldn't just read the works of others. I was going to have to start my own little ongoing serial. So I set out to write what was supposed to be a novella called *Pandemic*, about a virus called the Morningstar Strain that sweeps the globe and—naturally—zombifies its victims.

It got a positive response, so I kept adding to it. Pretty soon it had grown out of my control. It had reached novella length and had kept on going. I took it to its own site, made sure I kept a banner on the links page pointing people back to *Day by Day Armageddon*, and continued to add to it. Skip ahead a couple of years and *Pandemic* has become *Plague of the Dead*, a fully-fleshed out and published novel with two sequels in the works, and when you get down to the nitty-gritty, it's all because I stumbled onto *Day by Day Armageddon* and discovered the genre.

This story has everything that makes the genre near and dear to the hearts of its fans: stoic survivalism, slow, shambling undead, ever-present danger, a delightful sense of the gruesome and macabre, and of course, equipment lists.

Whether you're a true deadhead or just passing through the genre, this is one of those books that manages to grab your attention and keep you reading for no other reason than to find out what happens next—and that is the mark of a book worth reading. I say, any book that keeps you reading to find out some terrible secret, or keeps you turning pages because what's happening sickens you and you want it to end—those books aren't telling a story that's a rip-roaring good time. Those are the ones that'll leave you with an empty sense of apathy and disillusionment when you finish them. *Day by Day Armageddon* tells a story—and tells it well. When you're finished, you'll feel the blood pumping in your veins. You'll have just finished a great story. You'll feel alive—and that's more than most of the castmembers of the novel can say.

What more can be said besides "enjoy?" I can't think of a thing. So enjoy, reader. Enjoy.

Mahalo,

Z.A. RECHT

author of

PLAGUE OF THE DEAD

This Book is Dedicated to my
Brothers and Sisters in the
U.S. Military that have fought
and continue to fight the
Global War on Terror in Iraq,
Afghanistan and the
Republic of the Philippines
as well as the other dark and
unfamiliar corners of the earth.

In this world, I am no more.

I am a decadent monument of humanity.

I must strive for survival alone, afraid and vulnerable.

They are cold, recalcitrant and lethal, but I am alive.

---unknown survivor

In the Beginning...

January 1st

0358 hrs

Happy New Year to me. After a drunken night of fun, I sobered up and headed back home. I am so tired and bored of being home on vacation. I'm thankful for the break in training but Arkansas gets old quick. All my good friends are still drinking the same beer and doing the same thing. I will be extremely happy to get back home to San Antonio. New Year's resolution: start keeping a journal.

January 2nd

1100 hrs

My hangover is finally gone. I like to watch the news when I am near a television, but out here at my parent's house it seems that all they get are the local channels. I'm not going to attempt to try the dial up connection, as it will only frustrate me to the point of madness. I guess I will just check my e-mail when I get home. It seems that something is going on in China; the local news reported some type of influenza virus sweeping them over there. The flu season was bad here this year. I received my flu shot on base, avoiding the shortages of vaccine. I'm glad I get to go home tomorrow and get re-connected with my nice high speed Internet connection and digital cable.

My damn cell phone doesn't even work in this desolate place. The worst thing about being here is knowing I'm going to have to do a lot of flying to get back up to speed. When I signed up for naval aviation I didn't think it was going to involve constant work and studying just to stay competent.

January 3rd
0609 hrs

My grandmother called this morning to tell mom that we were going to war with China and to try to talk me into going to Canada to desert the military. I honestly think my grandmother has lost it. I turned on the news half expecting to see some kind of bullshit trade embargo deal with China. The news went on to say that President Bush has agreed to send medical military personnel over to China for consultation purposes only.

Makes me wonder, what do we have in America that a big bad country like China would need? They have all the natural resources anyone would want. I keep thinking I may have kept a light on in my house back in San Antonio. I have two small solar cell panels on my roof but I am wired to the electric grid. I just use the panels to sell electricity back to the utility company when I'm away on deployment. They have already paid for themselves.

January 5th
2004 hrs

After a nice ten-hour drive from NW Arkansas, I made it home yesterday. I received a satellite radio for Christmas and activated it for my trip home. I listened to BUZZ, or FOX all the way home with some music from my MP3 player thrown in every now and then. Wish I would have thought to hook the satellite radio up at my parent's house because I am almost certain that it would have worked out there even though it's in the middle of nowhere.

This China situation is starting to heat up. The news reports that we have lost over ten medical personnel to this China "bug." The other "military consultants" that are still in China are going to have to be quarantined prior to getting back to the United States. Talk about a pain in the ass. You go over there to help someone out and all you get in return is a prison sentence.

Today was not a bad Monday. Had to go fly a few sorties for training. The EP-3 is basically a C-130 with a lot of antennas. It's somewhat non-maneuverable, but it can receive some valuable data from 20,000 feet.

My friend in Groton, CT called today. Bryce is a Navy submarine officer. He really helped me out on a great deal on salvage parts off the old diesel boats when I was installing those panels in my house a few years back. He said that he was finally getting a divorce, she admitted to cheating on him. I kind of had a feeling about this girl, but I never said anything. Don't think it would have mattered if I did. We talked about this China thing for a long time and he seems to think it's some bad flu bug. I kind of think the same thing.

January 9th
1623 hrs

TGIF.

My mother called today on my cell worried asking me if I knew anything about what's going on overseas. I had to once again explain to my mother that just because I'm an officer in the Navy does not mean that I know who killed JFK or what happened in Roswell, NM. I love my mom, she just drives me nuts. I comforted her the best I could but something just isn't right. This nonsense is getting too much coverage in the news. I know the reporters smell a rat by the questions that they are asking FEMA and the Whitehouse and Homeland Defense.

The President made a speech (only available on AM band radio, probably to avoid to much publicity) and told the people that there is nothing to worry about and that the Army/Navy medical team in China had to send one of our doctors home because he was too ill to be left with the inadequate care/facilities in the location he was in. Another strange thing is that my squadron was scheduled to go to Atsugi, Japan next month for training in the Pacific and it was cancelled.

I asked my skipper about it, he just told me that they were trying not to take any chances with anything, and that there were rumors of "sick persons" in Honshu, Japan area. He gave me the nod and told me not to worry. Something doesn't sound right about this whole thing and it's starting to mess with my mind. I have a feeling I might want to go to the store and get some bottled water and things of that nature.

January 10th

0700 hrs

Not much sleep for me last night. I kept the news on all night just in case I missed anything. "I can assure the American people that we are taking every effort to contain this epidemic within the borders of China." Go ahead; say it in your best southern accent. I went to Wal-Mart today and bought a few things just in case I had to stay indoors to avoid getting sick. I bought some bottled water, canned beef stew and went by the base to chat with my supply friend at the warehouse. He told me that he could part with a few cases of MREs for a new nomex flight suit. Didn't bother me, I have a couple dozen of them. I picked out one of my lesser-worn flight suits and brought it to him. At least I will have a little variety in my diet if I need to stay home despite the fact that MREs are not an optimum bug out food because of how much they weigh and the excess space taken up by the packaging.

Vance (my supply connection) informed me he saw on an online government invoice, that a few thousand cases of MRE food were shipped to NORAD and a few other locations in the northwest. I asked him if it were normal, and he told me that these facilities haven't requested this much of a food supply since the Cuban missile crisis. I am thinking that if this is serious enough for the big wigs to want to lock themselves up for a few months it is more serious than I thought.

1042 hrs

I unloaded my "meals ready to eat" and noticed that one of the packages was busted. The smell of "Case A" MRE filled the air and reminded me of all of them that I had eaten when on station in the Arabian Gulf area on a ridiculous ground assignment. I hated it over there. It was so damn hot all the time, and when I had to embark on the ship it didn't make it any better. I checked my battery bank and all six batteries were in the green. Made me think of Bryce, and the "steal" I got on those old submarine batteries.

Back when submarines were diesel and not nuclear, they ran on batteries when under the water and when they surfaced they charged the batteries with a diesel generator. Some countries still use the old diesel boats. I thought this was a good idea, however, charging them with solar panels takes considerably longer, ten hours instead of three but the sun is free.

I miss my sisters, Jenny and Mandy. I haven't seen much of them since I have been in the service; they have sort of grown up on me. I called my dad's house and spoke to Jenny, the youngest. She was still half asleep when I called. I used to pick on her badly when she was little. Oh well, I love the little shit, and it builds character. Mandy is living back home, until she can get back on her feet again. Mandy has never been one to open up and talk to me about anything. I wish things would have been different, or that we would have been closer in our childhood.

I really need to clean my guns. Especially my CAR-15, she is really dirty. Might as well clean my pistols while I'm at it. While I'm on the subject, a few hundred rounds for the carbine is not a bad idea since it's so cheap. I don't exactly like looters, and if any of this quarantine shit comes this way, I want to be on the ball.

1436 hrs

Ok, I'm starting to worry, the Atlanta Center for Disease Control has reported a case of this "disease" at the Bethesda Naval Hospital in Maryland. Since there are no communists here to hush the news, the report got out. Apparently this disease causes the victim to lose some motor function, and also makes the victim seem to act erratic. I called in to the squadron to ask some questions. They told me that it's possible we might get Monday off so the Department of Defense can assess the threat to armed forces personnel inside the United States.

My mother also called about the news report and told me that the Bethesda Naval Hospital was the same hospital that they took Kennedy to when he was shot. I laughed at my mom's conspiracy theory attitude and told her to look after her husband (my stepfather) and try to avoid town if they already have enough supplies to stay put. I'm off to the local H.E.B. grocery store to get some stores, oh yeah, bought a thousand rounds for the carbine. Had to go to a few different stores to get them all. No one wanted to sell me that much all at once. It was probably some kind of liberal law that I didn't know about causing the red tape, or it could be a worried gun shop owner conserving some for himself and trying to keep his customers happy at the same time.

Almost out the door when I got the call to get in uniform and report to squadron H.Q. More to come.

1912 hrs

Just got back from my meeting at my squadron on base. I'm a little troubled. We got word that we have an important mission to fly tomorrow, on a Sunday. Apparently we are to fly recon over Atlanta, actually Decatur, Georgia. We are to focus on a specific area, namely the area around the CDC in Atlanta. It's nothing serious, we are just ordered to be a check and balance for the "G-men" in Washington, to make sure the CDC isn't hiding anything. It is just a photo recon, and signal recon mission.

Reminds me of the time I listened to my ex-girlfriend's phone conversation when I was flying training missions around the San Antonio area. I love the signals intelligence (SIGINT) equipment as it saved me a lot of money and time with that woman. Also in the news, one of the reporters was really punking out the Bethesda public affairs officer for not allowing press passage into the hospital to ask the medical personnel questions. O'rielly was asking..."What are you people hiding?" The young officer held her ground and insisted that it was just for the protection of the press corps that no extra personnel be admitted to the hospital, and besides it was not public property, it was a U.S. Government military hospital. Sort of odd that such a low ranking officer would be giving this type of interview.

January 11th

1944 hrs

I don't know what to think now. We were on station, sent to spy on our own government (CDC) at 0816 this morning. We started tuning our equipment to intercept any cell phone/land line/data transfer in or out of the CDC. I almost couldn't believe some of the things that were being said. There was an FBI agent on board, which is very unusual. During the brief prior to flight he stated it is technically illegal under Posse Comitatus for the military to be deployed inside the United States for official missions.

The agent was to be the official mission commander of the aircraft as to circumvent the military from being implicated for breaking any laws by operating inside the US. We were getting broken transmissions between the different CDC compounds about the virus being difficult to contain, and how the director of the CDC doesn't wish to look bad or in a bad light in front of the President. They were being as confidential as possible about this problem. They were using Secure Telephone Units (STU phones), but we had a little help from the National Security Agency so breaking the code was as easy as hitting decrypt on our proprietary software.

They went on to say that one of the infected males that they had quarantined had bitten a nurse in a fit of rage when she was trying to feed him. They had strapped him to his bed and put a mouthpiece in his mouth to avoid any further problems. The nurse wasn't doing so well and he had started to run a fever over the last few hours. The CDC voice also said, "Jim, (person on the other end) you wont believe the vital signs we are getting from the male." Jim said, "What do you mean, can you give me specifics?" CDC voice, "no, no specifics over the phone."

That is enough to start worrying for me. After we landed, I was forced to sign a non-disclosure agreement then I promptly broke it. I called my parents and told them what I thought they should do, then I started my own preparations. I found out we were not coming in tomorrow and that we were only required to call in by 0800 hrs.

I already cleaned up my rifle, so it was time to take care of the pistols. That brings my weapon number up to four firearms and a good knife. Went up on the roof to clean my solar cells, they were dingy and dusty. I also pulled up my notes on switching power from the power grid to submarine batteries, as it might prove useful in the future. I loaded all my magazines (10) for a total of 290 rounds. I never like to load the full thirty per magazine, as this could cause an inadvertent weapon jam.

My bottom floor windows are only double pane, so I went to the local super hardware store to purchase some DIY window bars for the two windows I have that are chest level. All others are too high to effectively reach without a ladder. I am going to install them now.

2354 hrs

I installed the bars using a tape measure, pencil, 5/32 drill bit, and a square head screwdriver (proprietary screwdriver that came with the bars and it's supposed to be difficult to get the screws out without using a drill.) If a looter is good enough to drill out my bars and take my shit while I'm still sleeping, I'll fucking load it on his truck for him.

While doing a quick walk around my yard perimeter, I have decided that my rock wall is not nearly high enough. Any able-bodied man could easily jump it. I had the wall built with the house. I have broken some bottles that I had in the spare room and I used some bonding cement to glue the shards around the top of my wall perimeter every foot or so. At least it might slow someone down. I was listening to my headset radio while I worked and now that I am more informed, I can only see the situation getting worse.

The radio says that the president is issuing a statement in the morning at 0900 EST. Down the street in the distance I can see a family packing up the SUV and leaving. No one takes vacations this time of year so I can only infer that they are bugging out. I'm going to get more supplies tomorrow after I listen to the president's speech and call in to my squadron to check in.

January 12th

0934 hrs

All I can say is, wow. The President pretty much said that the disease is highly contagious and there is no cure at this time. He said that Americans are encouraged to stay indoors and to report anyone with "suspicious symptoms" to the authorities at once. One of the press cronies managed to get a question in and asked, "Mr. President! Mr. President! Could you please elaborate on suspicious symptoms?" The President replied that we should be on the look out for person or persons acting wildly and looking ill.

He also said, "It is extremely important that if any of our family members have these symptoms it is paramount that you give them no special treatment, turn them in just as you would a stranger with the same symptoms."

A 1-800 number flashed on the screen and he then said:

"I urge you to call this number in the event that there are any outbreak symptoms in your community. We have specially trained men and women to handle the situation, we will take your loved ones to a suitable medical facility for treatment."

The President also said that he is ordering a full withdrawal of American military and civilians in China and Iraq. He commented that he was considering withdrawing troops from the DMZ in South Korea. A video clip played in the background showing the U.S. Embassy in China being evacuated under the close supervision of heavily armed U.S. Marines. One of the clips showed three Marines taking down the American flag to signify that the embassy was officially decommissioned. A scene not unlike the fall of Saigon flashed on to the screen. There were mobs of U.S. citizens being evacuated via helicopter from a random rooftop in Beijing. There were sounds of automatic weapons in the background but the people on the roof didn't seem concerned, they just wanted out. I'm off to get supplies.

1522 hrs

It was a total mad house. I got into an accident in the parking lot at the hardware store, and some lady almost fought me for the (4) five gallon barrels of water that I bought at Wal-Mart. I also bought some more 9mm rounds while I was there. I am happy that I have a few cases of MREs and enough water to sustain me in case this gets worse. I also bought some cheap throwaway facemask to wear in case there are any outbreaks at my location. I bought what was left on the shelf in the canned goods section. I purchased fifty cans of different soups. I can't believe this. I haven't felt this surreal since 9/11.

My parents are safe out in the hills of Arkansas, I advised them to stay home and don't go into town for anything. They always have a freshly stocked freezer, and water is not an issue since they use well water. They have a small generator for electricity in the winter when the power lines freeze and break.

I bought some hardware at one of the major hardware chains; some boards for general purpose and some heavy steel brackets and bolts to install a primitive barricade on my front and back doors. It was just a simple 4x4 board sliding into a rest on the inside of my door to keep anyone from smashing their way in. I think that if I ration myself to one liter per day and 1000-1500 calorie diet, I could last for at least five months on my current supply of food.

I also turned on the citizen band radio today to see who was on. I selected channel nineteen to hear what the truckers had to say about all this. They were generally angry about all the roadblocks and cargo searches they were experiencing. Apparently the CDC and INS were concerned about semi trucks carrying a truckload of illegal immigrants in the trailer over the border. Something about it not being safe and that they had an incident of a case of this bug when an INS agent opened gate to the back of another trucker's trailer.

According to what I was hearing, they had to quarantine the whole truck and the agent on duty because every damn person in the back was infected and one of the infected immigrants attacked the agent, probably scared of going back to Mexico. I'm going to call one of my Marine buddies out in San Diego to see what he is doing about all this.

1854 hrs

I just got off the phone with my buddy Shep in the Marines. He said that there were armed National Guardsmen on the street corners in San Diego and that he was being called in to be a part of his base's security team. He told me that he was told to move his wife on base to the cold war shelter that was being reopened and that they were going to close the gates and quarantine the base in the event that there was an outbreak in that area. The sun is down now. I have motion sensor lights on my house around the perimeter. In the event a looter sneaks over and tries to steal anything, at least the light will go on. When I go to sleep tonight, I will sleep with the Glock under my pillow and the CAR-15 next to my bed.

The news is going on about reports of strange phenomenon reported in the major cities, apparently some cases of cannibalism have been reported. That is America for you. The shit hits the fan and everyone goes crazy. Since I happen to live in the outskirts of the eighth largest city in the nation, this news isn't good news. I hear police and ambulance sirens going up and down the street outside my wall. I'm hungry but I have already had too much to eat today. Celery fits the bill I suppose.

2113 hrs

CNN is reporting with a web camera in Times Square. Apparently they own it and the feds haven't thought to have it shut down. They are panning it around and the grainy images are showing armed military troops shooting civilians. Damn, there are going to be some lawsuits over this one.

The image was quickly cut-off by the emergency broadcast system. After a few minutes the picture came in as the Secretary of Homeland Defense stepped up to a podium marked with the seal of the President.

"America, I'm sorry to report that despite our best efforts, this disease has broken the bonds of our containment measures. It is no longer safe to inhabit larger cities. Safe zones are being set up on the outskirts of high population areas and will be open to those not infected with this disease. Please try to remain calm, as what I'm about to say will sound quite abominable. This disease is reportedly transmitted by the bite from one of the infected. We are not sure if this is linked to saliva, blood or both. The infected soon succumb to their wound and expire, only to rise within the hour and seek out living humans. It is not known why those who die of natural causes are returning; however this is also the case. I apologize that the President could not be here, as he is being transferred to a secure location. May God be with us all in this trying time. I now turn you over to General Meyers."

As soon as the Homeland Defense Secretary began to close his folder, he was bombarded with questions from the press corps below the stage. It was more like Wall Street trading than a press conference. Even though you couldn't see the crowd of press in front of the podium, you could feel them there by the ambient noise, camera flashes, and garbled voices. One of the particularly alarming question and answer included one of the reporters asking how the Secretary knew the creatures were dead or if they were merely infected with a disease. The Secretary replied by saying, "Living humans don't have ambient body temperatures that match the ambient air temperature. This morning we locked one of the creatures in a lab reefer. We have recorded a sustained body temperature at 40 degrees Fahrenheit for over twelve hours and counting."

The crowd gasped at this in disbelief and more questions poured toward the podium. "What are the chances of being infected by a bite?" The secretary took a deep breath and said, "So far the communicability of this disease is one hundred percent post-attack if the skin is broken by a bite." I can't fucking believe this is happening. I am calling my family.

2200 hrs

After trying to call for over thirty minutes, I realized that that's exactly what everyone else in the United States is doing. The phone lines can't handle that kind of usage. I tried my mobile phone. Same results. "Network busy." I also listened to what the General had to say during my redial attempts.

"The best defense in this situation is to remain in your home and await the evacuation teams. Avoid infected personnel at all costs. If you are forced into an altercation with one of these individuals, the only thing that will have effect is trauma to the cranium. If you are unfortunate enough to be forced to defend yourself from a loved one, do so with same vigilance you would a stranger, as that is what he or she is. Try your best to avoid getting bitten as there is no way to avoid infection by these means.
The reports coming in from our troops returning from China indicate that the creatures are primarily attracted to loud noises. It seems they use this as a primary method for finding prey. I must stress that it is in your best interest to remain indoors and to remain quiet and calm. Our best guess from our CIA human intelligence (HUMINT) operators on the ground in China is that the disease has been rampant in China for more than three weeks and they are in a state of disaster. If we don't do things differently than the Chinese did we could be doomed to the same fate."

The General was then ushered off the podium and given a stern glance by one of the civilian government officials. What followed next was an attempt by one of the speakers to apply a calm tone to what the General had relayed.

I'm scared...I really don't know what else to do other than turn the lights out sit here and write...my rifle is slung over my shoulder even as I sit here...There is a knock at the door. Back soon...

2350 hrs

One of my fellow officers from the squadron came over to tell me about the rumors he had heard from Jake, our mutual friend when Jake had returned from a mission over one of the outbreak areas in Atlanta, GA. During the mission Jake said that he had seen numerous infected corpses walking the streets in the south part of town. He said he could see the stray dogs barking at them in the streets and watched as the infected tried to lunge at the dogs. He was using the camera pod to digitally zoom in. To him it seemed like some of the younger gang members were trying to take law into their own hands by shooting the infected corpses.

From what my friend said, Jake was as white as a ghost when he landed, not believing what his eyes had transmitted to his brain. Chris, my midnight visitor was scared from what Jake had told him, I could see it in his eyes. He asked if I wanted to come with him and stay on the base in the shelter that they had organized. I knew what he was talking about. On the base there are numerous cold war bomb shelters still active and mostly being used to store civil defense food and water and various medical supplies. I looked at Chris and told him that he would be ok, just keep a level head and watch his back.

I told him that I was going to stay here alone and try to keep out of view of anybody and anything. He asked me if I was sure, I told him yes. He left and I'm tired. Going to lock it up and watch some news then TRY to get some sleep. I still can't believe this. Part of me wants to see for myself, part of me wants to just hide under the table with my guns and shiver.

January 13th

1143 hrs

No sleep came for me last night. I kept hearing police and ambulance sirens and fire trucks. Very disturbing. Thought I could hear gunshots in the distance, but it could have been vehicle backfire. Got out of bed at 0500 hrs. Went to the garage to get the florescent bulbs for perimeter and inside lights. I normally use regular bulbs because they are a little brighter, but given my situation, I may have to temporarily live off solar/battery power if any fires knock out the transformers or power grid.

The news is only portraying death doom and destruction. The news is now saying that every major city is reporting cases of the dead walking. This morning I began boarding up all my windows, even the ones that are not on ground level. I also boarded up the two vulnerable windows that I recently installed bars on, just in case. I feel pretty safe about the windows. I put the efficient bulbs on my perimeter lights.

Disadvantage: It takes them a couple of seconds to come on when the motion sensor trips.

Advantage: Will not drain my deep-cycle batteries as quickly.

I'm concerned about my safety, but I am taking every precaution to ensure that I am doing ok. I'm making a new section for supplies so that I can keep track of the amount of water and food I am consuming. I also checked the acid level of my batteries. They are good to go. Should last through this, unless...well I don't want to go there in my mind right now.

1555 hrs

I finally got through to my Mother and Stepfather (Dad). Mom was hysterical. I had to talk to dad to get any words in. He told me that things were fine and that they were as safe as possible. They hadn't seen any signs of the disease, but told me that there were reports in town of possible outbreak (10 miles away).

They had the guns and dogs ready for looters if the situation should arise. I asked dad what his plans were if things got too bad at home. He said that he and mom and the dogs would probably head out to Fincher cave if things got too bad. It is just a small cave that I used to play in when I was young. Old man Fincher used to threaten to shoot me with his rock salt loaded twelve gauge if I kept trespassing in his cave without my parents. That seems like ages ago. I was only twelve then. I told them that I would stay in touch as long as the lines were up. It was no use with the cell phone as it was already dead. The high maintenance services would be the first to go.

1910 hrs

The lights were flickering today. Not a normal occurrence here. I was cleaning my rifle when it happened. I thought they were going to go out, but they held. Sirens and gunshots can be heard in the wind. That sums most of the sounds I heard today. After I got of the phone with my family (decided to call my Dad, no answer), I also started preparations to keep my house from looking too inhabited.

I took the staple gun and some extra blankets and gunned them over my re-enforced windows to make sure no ambient light gets out when I check the TV for news or turn on a light, or use my computer. I have a couple old batteries left over from my last laptop. Not the same model as my Apple, but I could get it to work with some electrical wire if I had to. I'm just thinking worse case. I used some duct tape and wired my web cam to overlook my front yard so instead of opening curtains to look outside, I could just look in my screen.

When my computer is in sleep mode (clamshell closed), I can't even see the needles move on my drain gauge of my battery bank. I had to use my extra USB cable from my printer, but who really cares about printing anything at a time like this. It's not like I'm going to be printing pizza coupons. I sent out some e-mails but got them all back. There were numerous error messages stating that server (insert random IP) was down. It's dark here now. I would get my camera out and take a picture outside my upstairs window. I'm just too scared.

2319 hrs

I woke up to the sounds of gunshots nearer this time and turned the cam on. Looks like a green Army transport truck parked under a street light on the corner in front of my house. There are soldiers loading a body in the back of the truck. I have to sleep tonight. Perimeter is secure...I just took the risk of taking an off-the-shelf sleep aid (just 1/2 dose) to try to cut the edge off. The news says that martial law is in effect in the inner city. I'm on the outskirts. It could be put into effect here too if these Army guys keep showing up. Oh yeah, I got a call from the squadron today, I didn't answer. It was my Executive Officer telling me I had to report to the shelter and to call him immediately upon receipt of his message. Yeah right, fuck you sir...feeling the effects of sleepiness...

January 14th

0815 hrs

I fell asleep to the sound of ocean tides on my mp3 player. I turned it up to drown out some of the noise. Woke up around 0300 to take a piss. I actually forgot what was going on. It reminded me of my childhood and early adulthood when something bad would happen, like a death in the family. There were brief moments of levity where my mind would forget the tragedy and then the cold hard facts would hit me. The second my hand reached out to turn on the television the tragedy returned to my conscious thought. I watched as endless talking heads were giving their theory on the cause and effect. The stock market is to the point of non-recovery.

The Coast Guard's helicopter fleet has been reassigned inland to aid law enforcement and military personnel evacuate some of the harder hit areas. A news clip that really got to me in particular, showed a group of survivors on a rooftop in San Diego. The helicopter was circling the roof of the building and I could see the wind from the helicopter rotors blowing the people's hair and clothes around. The people were trapped on top of a large air conditioning unit; apparently they had climbed up there to escape their pursuers (a dozen walking corpses). A particular shocking image was that of a mother and her daughter. The mother had her daughter's mouth taped over and her hands and feet bound. She wasn't one of us anymore. The daughter was dead. The mother just couldn't let go. The poor ignorant woman.

I don't know how to react to seeing the world crumble. There are countless cities scrolling by on the news tickers. Even my own city made its way across the bottom of the screen. There are no commercials on the television, only the talking heads.

Reporter: "The following scenes display material that is not suitable for young children."

The scene showed a group of reporters in their news van driving through downtown Chicago. The camera was pointing to the driver and you could see that he was visibly shaken and trying his best to keep the van on the road. The camera then panned to a frontal view. There are seas of figures in front and on the sides of the van. I could tell the van was moving as quickly as it could. You could hear a male voice crying from the back of the van. The driver did his best to weave in and out, but there were just to many bodies walking into the van to avoid. The camera panned back to the rear seat to get a shot of the female reporter.

She said, "As you can see, it would be SUICIDE to enter the city of Chicago, may god help us all."

She then made a "cut-throat" gesture and the camera cut out. The screen went back to the reporter. He made a half-hearted statement about hoping they would return safely, all the while trying to keep up a fake smile. I turned off the TV and made my own assessment outside my house.

0900 hrs

→ Perimeter wall: solid

→ Street view: Emergency vehicles only. I see some human figures, but can't tell friend or foe.

→ Threats: I see a fire burning in the distance about a mile up the road. I can tell by direction of smoke that it's blowing away from me.

2212 hrs

I came across a post on a survivalist forum online. I guess the news isn't reporting the whole truth. A sailor holding out on a U.S. Naval warship posted today. Apparently he is living off fish and seagulls. I hope he makes it. This just reassures my thought that the government is and will continue to hide the facts. This brings up a question. What government? I haven't seen any representatives of the White House on the TV in over 24 hours.

I spent the rest of the morning and afternoon prepping my backpack with a "bug-out" kit, in the event I have to get the fuck out of Dodge, and also filling up the bathtubs in my house. The water hasn't shut off yet so I'm going to start drinking out of the tub to conserve my bottled water. I began rationing food today. Only had a can of stew and a banana. Might as well eat all the fruit now because it will be useless within a week (sans the apples). I checked the perimeter again, and decided that I will keep my flight suit on at all times and remain as camouflaged as possible when I go out.

I have a nomex mask and gloves and ten nomex flight suits. I think it's a good idea to wear the flight suit because:

1. They are fireproof, and
2. They are one piece and no hassle, which means less to get snagged on shit if I have to get on the run. The only bad thing is that I need to be in a very safe place if I need to use the head.

I fashioned a pretty good washboard from the grill part of my propane grill. Had to wire brush it clean, but it will serve a good purpose in keeping my clothes clean and giving me less of a chance of catching disease or rash. I'm going to shave every other day to save on razors.

2350 hrs

I heard movement outside my gates and disabled the motion sensor lights while putting on my mask and gloves. I grabbed my rifle and went outside to investigate the area. I saw a strange man in civilian clothes stumbling up the street bumping into my rock wall at random intervals. Looked a lot like those corpses on the TV (the way he walked). I'm not taking any chances, nor am I going to get "commando" fever. I shall remain silent too avoid being seen or heard by anything alive or dead. Besides, it was too dark to tell whether or not he was alive or dead. I feel like a fucking idiot for not stealing some NVGs from the squadron when I had the chance. They would be handy in this situation. Good night journal.

January 15th

2237 hrs

I spent the whole day monitoring the situation outside my home. I saw some of the poor bastards shuffling up the street around 1045 this morning. I used my binoculars to get a decent view. Some of the ashen bodies looked normal, some of them not so normal. One of them had its throat torn out. Very unsettling. My phone rang today around noon (it was out momentarily earlier). I had set it to quiet mode a couple days ago. I was sitting next to it, so I decided to pick it up, half expecting it to be one of my superiors wondering why I'm not on the base in the shelter. It was one of my squadron buddies, Jake. We went through Officer Candidate School together.

Surprisingly enough, we both picked the same profession, and ended up the same places. He was telling me the situation on base, and I can say that I made a good decision by staying here. He told me that he was sent to pick up some blankets from the base storage units near the west gate. When he arrived he said that the military police were constantly shooting over the fence at the creatures in an effort to weed out some of the mass before it was too much for the gate to handle. A Humvee with a .50 cal was dispatched to deal with the crowd but they had to retreat when the gunner almost got pulled off the vehicle.

He said he didn't know how long the gates would hold, but he was sure that they couldn't get by the concrete bomb shelter. I asked him from where he was calling. He told me that he was calling the base's DSN lines (lines strictly for DOD use). He said that the officers were all heavily armed in the bunker and that he thought they had enough food for at least a few weeks. I told him not to worry about me, and that no one knows I'm even here. Instant Karma was playing in the background. That is all for today, journal.

January 16th
2200 hrs

The phones are dead again. At least the broadband is still working. All the news websites have stopped putting up the nice colorful flash images and are just sticking to basic tickers. I suppose they don't have time to be fancy. I spent the day preparing, loading up some bottled water and one case of MREs to the attic just in case. I also took some plywood from the garage and made a temporary floor up there big enough to sleep on. No emergency vehicles today. The air was thick with smoke from fires in the city. I can see the fires outside now even through the rain. All the lights are off in my house. The electricity kept flickering again today. If the electricity goes out all together, it will take me at least twenty minutes to set up for solar/ battery power "off grid."

The news isn't even broadcasting live anymore on TV. It's obvious they are controlling the broadcast remotely because all you see are street corner cameras that are only connected to the world through the WWW. Oh, and the tickers on the screen keep rolling by showing government shelter centers. Half of it is misspelled and hastily typed, not unlike this journal. One camera of particular interest was a traffic camera pointing at a random interstate in California. It showed those dead bastards trapped in their vehicles with their seat belts still on trying to scratch and moan their way out. From the looks of it, they died in an accident and came back only to be stuck in a car with no motor skills to unfasten the seatbelt. That makes me feel better, because if they can't un-click the belt, they can't turn the doorknob.

<u>Theory:</u> Phones down, Internet up...why? I think it's because most of the lines dealing with the Internet are buried or satellite. Most of the phone lines are above ground and susceptible to fire and weather.

January 17th
1424 hrs

The sun is out. It is getting hot indoors. I don't want to run the air conditioner out of fear of the noise it will make. Electricity is intermittent. Water pressure is failing. I'm keeping the tubs filled up as I drink water. I'm not risking a shower or bath because I will have to drain the water to do this and I might lose total pressure. Using a bucket and sponge to take a bath. Trying to shave every other day to keep my morale up. The same news keeps flashing on the screen. No reporters in two days. I'm trying to establish a routine as to maintain sanity. In the early AM I am walking the perimeter before the sun rises as to avoid attention from those things. Later in the AM I intend to work out by doing basic calisthenics.

I had a real scare this morning. A cat had jumped my fence in order to avoid being killed by one of those things. I didn't think much of it until the cat had ran off and jumped the fence opposite the side it came in on. That's when the thing that was pursuing it decided it wanted to keep up the chase. I could only see its hands as it groped over the fence feeling for the cat. It just kept cutting itself on the broken glass that I had glued there a few days earlier. I guess these things have no fear of pain.

I think it got angry because it started beating on my wall. I could hear the thuds from the other side. Let it thud away I suppose it's going to take a lot more than that to tear down my rock wall. There are four or five of them in that area now. They are shambling around. I get a feeling they sense I'm here, but I cannot be sure. If it gets too bad, I will have to deal with them. I was thinking I might get my stepladder and some of my reserve kerosene and put it in my pesticide sprayer. I will climb the ladder and spray them down then light a match and burn them to death, again. It's much quieter than shooting them I suppose. At least this way I will be able to get a good look at one of them. I'm off to make preparations for this.

1600 hrs

I cannot begin to describe how disgusting these things look. I am a believer now. They are certainly dead and certainly want me to be dead with them. I quietly went to the garage to get my kerosene, ladder and sprayer. I set the ladder up first. Went over to the section that I thought they were near. I could hear footsteps where I placed the ladder.

I wanted so bad to see, but I was scared to look. I went back to the garage, and picked up the rest of my death squad gear. I could have easily shot them, but I don't want to make the noise, or waste the ammunition. I filled the sprayer up and climbed the ladder. First rung...I could see the tops of three of their heads...second rung, they noticed my presence and this awful gurgling moaning sound erupted from one of them. Sounded like, well I don't know what it sounded like. I got to the top of the ladder and there were six of them gathered around my position on the opposite side of the wall.

I pumped the canister to get pressure to the sprayer and doused the bastards with kerosene. They were fucking pissed, or hungry, or both, I don't know. I lit a match and threw it at the closest one, no dice, didn't ignite. I repeated this three more times as these vicious things kept clawing at the wall trying to get to me. Finally on the fourth attempt one of them caught fire. I knew I had to stay there on the ladder so I could make them bump into each other and spread the fire.

Finally when they were all up in flames, I stepped down from the ladder and put away my gear. I could hear the popping sound of burning fat for the next two hours. I'm glad it had rained for the past few days, or I wouldn't have even thought about doing this. I really have to start making a back up plan in the event I get SNAFU'ed here at my house.

1. They feel no pain.
2. They want to eat me.
3. Fire re-kills them.
4. Not sure about small arms fire yet.

1815 hrs

The sun is quickly going down. From my laptop web cam, I can see numerous figures up the street gathering around another house. I wonder if someone is alive in there? I hear birds going crazy in that direction. Not sure what the deal is. I hope if someone is alive in there, they have the common sense to stay quiet, because I really don't want to find out how gunfire affects them just yet. I don't want to be a hero today. I miss the world already. I miss flying. I miss being a Naval officer. I guess I still am, but I'm not sure if there is even a government around to recognize my commission. I sharpened my knife to a honed perfection today. It was sort of a relaxation technique. Also cleaned my carbine, although she didn't need it. A visual inspection was made of all weapons.

The solar panels are running efficiently. I dread going on the roof to clean them, because I'm sure I will be spotted. I should do it at night. That's a ways off. I heard the sound of a helicopter today, didn't take the chance to go outside and look even though those things can't spot me from ground level. Maybe they can smell me. It makes me wonder what senses they lost or gained from dying and coming back. I think it probably took longer than normal for the ones that I burned to die, as compared to a normal human.

I saw the caps of the flames from my house over the wall stumbling around for at least three minutes. The average human would collapse from pain in less than thirty seconds, I would guess. When it gets dark, I am going to use the LASER sight on my pistol to try to signal the house up the street. At least that way the creatures will not see the signal, only the recipient will if they exist or are even alive.

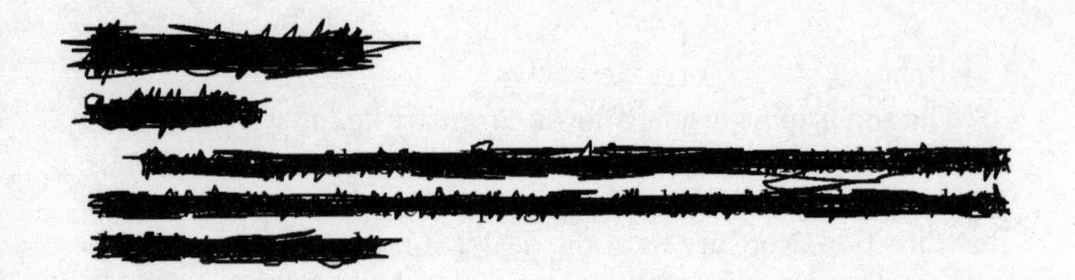

John

2251 hrs

Using my pistol LASER sight, I made the attempt at signaling the house that the creatures were gathering around. At first I just aimed the "dot" at every window and shook it around. After about five minutes of this, I saw the faint glow of a flashlight in the upstairs window. Whomever it was started flashing the light. "Dit-dit-dit-da-da-da-dit-dit-dit." It was SOS in Morse code. I learned Morse code a few years back at a military radioman school I attended and was pretty good at visually interpreting and pretty shitty at interpreting it through audio means.

This time I was in luck. I grabbed a pencil and some scratch paper (bills that I will never pay) and gave the signal that I was ready to copy. The things weren't reacting to the other person's flashlight, so I decided to use my L.E.D. light because of the 25 hours of battery life, unlike my pistol laser sight. I started to copy the Morse. At first it was slow going because I had to signal him/her to repeat the signal. I got into the groove after a couple of sentences.

O...K...(break)
H...E...R...E...(break)...N...A...M...E...(break)
....J...O...H...N...(break)...
Y...O...U...?(interrogative)

I told him my name and that I was OK also. I also told him to be quiet, the things like sound. He understood. Not bad communication for being a hundred yards away. He signaled and said that his house was secure and that he had a plan to make communication faster, but it would wait until tomorrow. I asked him what the plan involved his reply was:

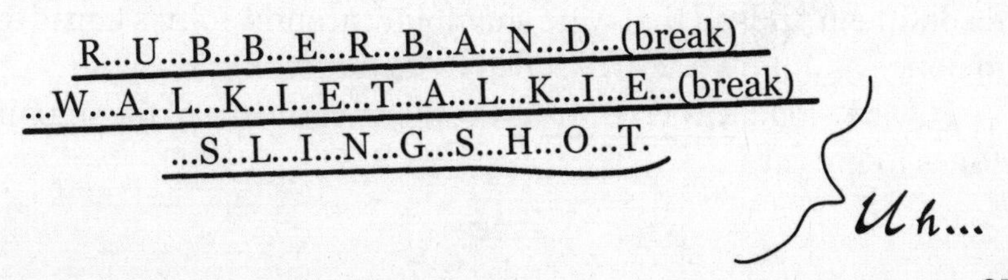

I told John that I sort of understood. He signaled that it was time for him to get some rest. I let him go after that. That was over an hour ago and I still cannot fathom what he intends to do with a rubber band, a small radio and a slingshot. I can't think of a sling shot big enough to propel a hand held walk & talk one hundred yards to my house and even if it could, it would break into a million pieces if it did make it over here. I guess at least I have something to look forward to for tomorrow.

January 18th

1012 hrs

I woke up at 0605 and went to look out the upstairs window. Sat there for a minute with my light and then began to try and hail John. I kept flashing my light at the window. No answer. I started thinking the worst. I just sat there for a few minutes feeling sad, knowing that in half an hour it wouldn't matter anyway because the sun would be too bright for us to see each others flashing signal. That was when I saw him. I saw movement on the roof, the silhouette of a middle-aged man in a plaid button up red and black shirt and jeans. I grabbed my binoculars ran back and started flashing my light.

The sun was starting to shine so I was not sure if he could see the light trying to compete with the sun's brightness. He looked my direction and waved. Then he held up this long green elastic looking thing and what looked like a short stubby metal coffee thermos.

He then proceeded to wrap one end of the green band around the chimney and the other around his exterior attic fan, forming a primitive sling. He put the thermos in the sling and started walking down the other side of his roof, out of my sight stretching the green looking band. It seemed like a long time. Finally, I saw the band snap upwards, then less than a second later, when the sound caught up, I heard the snap.

The thermos that John had cradled into the band was shooting at a trajectory that would put it roughly somewhere in my yard. The ten or fifteen undead that were shambling around John's house took no notice as John's package sailed to its target.

I heard a loud KA-THUMP as the thermos hit one of the stepping-stones in my yard.

The package had made it over 100 yards inside the perimeter of my fence. Not without cost though. The sound was loud and two of the things turned from John's house, as if they heard it and started walking in my general direction. I wasted no time and immediately put my gloves and mask on and grabbed my pistol. I didn't feel it necessary to bring the rifle for a front yard expedition.

I made it to ground zero in less than fifteen seconds, picked up the dented thermos and ran back inside waving at John. He could see me and I could see him, but the things could see neither of us from our positions. When I got inside I opened John's package and found two packages of eight triple 'A' Duracell batteries, and the following two items: a note from John, and a two-way radio.

NEIGHBOR,
Signal me back
on channel Ø7.
-John
P.S. I told
you it would work!

It also came stuffed with packing foam peanuts.

The corpses finally made it to my general area, but the sound of the impact was so brief they had no idea what specific area to go to. I loaded the batteries (takes 4 AAA) into the two-way radio and put the ear bud on. John was already trying to get me on channel seven. We talked for a great while. He told me that he used his wife's yoga resistance band to slingshot the thermos. We both laughed at that. I was afraid to ask him about his wife so instead I asked him if he had lost anyone in all this, he simply replied, "I think everyone has."

I didn't probe any further. I asked him what his plans were, and what his supplies looked like. He told me that he was still formulating a plan of survival and a backup of escape, and that he had plenty of food and water. He also told me that he had a semi-automatic .22 rifle and a couple bricks of ammunition. Hell, that's more ammo than I have.

I asked him why all of them were gathered around his house and he told me that it was because of his dog, she started barking at a group of them so he had to muzzle her. I asked what kind of dog he had, and he told me that he had an Italian greyhound (tiny version of regular greyhound) named Annabelle. I was jealous of the companionship he had. My busy Navy schedule kept me from getting a pet, because I would deploy at odd times. I told him that I had another friend named John back at the squadron. He said that we should conserve battery power and think of something useful to chat about in the evening and that he would be back on at 1800 sharp. I agreed and we both signed off.

(1.) Supplies: status GOOD !

1950 hrs

John was on the air and ready at 1800 just like he said. We spoke about our current situation and came up with theories of how it began. I asked John if he knew if bullets could kill them, he was not sure. I told him about my little campfire yesterday and he told me he saw the fire after they had succumbed and wondered what happened. He finally broke the news to me about his wife. His son was away for college at Purdue when all of this hit. His wife was a victim of one of those things. It had attacked just before sunset days earlier as she walked out to the shed to get some nails for the boards they were putting up. It was a bum that had died the night before after taking refuge in the backyard shed. By the time his wife called out, it was too late. When he arrived with a baseball bat she was gripping her bloody arm and running toward him with the creature behind her. He killed it with the bat.

He said that the bite on the arm immediately showed signs of infection and swelling. Black and red vein tracks were spreading toward her shoulder within an hour. He applied first aid and kept her comfortable, but there was nothing else he could do. He started to cry, (I could hear his tears through the tinny transmission of the 2-way) and I tried to change the subject, he said "I had to put her down, it hurt like hell, but I had to." I told him not to think about this and try to keep his head in the game for the time being. He agreed and we kept talking.

I told him that I had seen numerous postings from survivors all over the United States on the Internet, but none from our allies overseas. He asked me to read them to him so I did. I told him that one survivor was in southeast Texas, so that means that he and I weren't the last survivors here. I read about the survivor from New York and John told me in a distant voice that he had family there. We both went off the air for a couple minutes to get our road atlases.

We got back on and started to discuss escape routes should this area become infested and uninhabitable. He suggested the Alamo because it's only a half a day's walk from here. I told him that I thought it would be suicide to enter the city now. I suggested that we "borrow" a sturdy vehicle and head east to the Gulf of Mexico and find an offshore oilrig.

John said that his power had been flickering on and off in the past few days and he wasn't sure how long it would hold. John had a Honda generator in his basement, but he told me he refused to use it unless he had to, because it might be audible outside. We decided not to waste too much battery power on these two-way radios. I only had three other sets of triple A's.

I tried the CB radio on every channel, only static.

I'm hungry.

<u>Thought</u>: I still have my satellite radio in my vehicle.

→ Satellite = no lines to catch on fire. If the uplink station is still operational someone could uplink from the WWW, and transmit. I will go out tonight and get the radio and UHF antenna.

2334 hrs

John and I decided that if we needed to talk to one another we would be at the window at the top of the hour to flash our lights. We decided to make a deal to go to the window and check on each other every hour, until we signaled it was time for bed (5) flashes. No light means there is no need to waste our two-way radio batteries. I checked my radio. It seems to work fine; unfortunately every station that is active is playing a constant loop. Some of the news channels are broadcasting stories and news from last week. Old news. I will continue to monitor when I can. I checked the CB radio again. I could have sworn that I heard the faint signal of a human voice. I called out and tried to get a response, no joy.

Looking out the window, I see at least a dozen fires in the distance, and every now and again, I think I hear gunfire. I imagined for a moment that it could be the last survivors in the big city. I bet it is a war zone there. I feel dirty, but I just don't want to waste the water. That reminded me to check the water pressure. Still some left. I haven't left the confines of my domicile for five days I think (sans the bonfire and slingshot incident). It feels like a month.

I wonder how other countries are holding up. I bet Eskimos and some of the small islands in the Philippines aren't really affected by this. Lucky bastards. I wonder if the walking dead are cold to the touch? That would lead me to believe that they don't generate body heat therefore they are much like a snake. I theorize that if it gets very cold, they may slow down. Tomorrow is Sunday. No church for me tomorrow. I guess he wasn't bullshitting about the Omega part in the book of Revelations. It's almost midnight, so I'm off to give my (5) flashes to John.

January 19th
1659 hrs

I woke up this morning to no power. It was around 0730. At 0800 sharp I went to the window to signal John. He was already there. He told me that the power went out last night at about 0330. I slept right through it. I don't know what it is, but I have just been able to sleep a little better since I met John. I guess it's the feeling of not being alone. Being in the military I never got a chance to make many close friends because I would always be on the move. That was the case here. I had this house built because I thought it would be a good investment and because I knew I would be here for a couple years.

John said that he really didn't need any power to do anything. He had a propane cooker and plenty of water. I told him that I was using solar power with deep cycle submarine batteries.

My broadband connection is running through the buried cable lines, and it still seems to be unaffected. There is also power to the phone grid because when I pick the phone up, I get the quick busy tone telling me the switchboards are down, but the lines are not out. I told John that I would be back soon and that I had to go to the garage to switch from the power grid to my own power supply (wouldn't want the power surging back on and damaging my battery banks).

After I switched power to solar/battery, I got back on the horn with John. He asked if there were any new survivor entries on the online forums and I read them to him. People from all over the US were sounding off. Some sounded bleak, others sounded hopeful. I guess reading the survivor entries to John was sort of an outlet. John and I discussed travel. I told John that I could fly. If I had a way to get an operational aircraft, we could make it pretty much anywhere in the US, as long as we had the charts so that I could find airfields with fuel. We were both getting cabin fever and it showed. We were just thinking of excuses to leave this dead place.

1920 hrs

Gunshots outside. It's too dark to see John's house without the streetlight. I turned my radio on and waited for a few minutes. I was sure John was in danger until I heard him crackle in. "Don't worry, I'm safe, I had to shoot some of them because they were starting to pile up onto each other and form a human ladder." I asked him how they were affected by the shots. He said that he shot twelve of them in the head using only the moonlight at close range and killed them. That's good news. I know that those shots are going to attract more of them, so I will be sleeping extra softly tonight. Suggested to John that he be ready at first light to kill twice as many as he killed today.

2311 hrs

I can't really sleep as I keep thinking about all the people left alive and struggling to survive. A woman in Oklahoma is trapped with her children, and asking for advice on the online message boards. What grief it would bring me to find out that my advice doomed someone to being destroyed by a crowd of those things? I know that if I was in a situation...trapped...with the undead increasing in numbers daily around my perimeter that I would have no choice but to leave. I'm thinking of short-term safe havens as we speak. Water towers, train cars (with roof exits), roofs of buildings with limited roof access come to mind. I just wouldn't want to be somewhere surrounded with no way out. If there are any prisons or military facilities, I might choose those. They are defensible if, and only if you can clear them out. The more I think about it, the more I realize that my situation could become much like hers quickly if I don't stay in the game. I don't feel it prudent to give others advice, as I am no expert. I just hope that we all survive. There doesn't seem to be much chance for most of them.

The Marriage of Figaro

January 20th
2223 hrs

Situation, dire...John and I woke up today and started communicating on the two ways. What I saw out the window was almost too much. It was 0700 hrs and there were approximately one hundred of those things on our street forming a human moat around John's house. I grabbed my carbine, checked its action, holstered my side arm and prepared for battle. I donned gloves, hood, and flight suit, and John's radio with ear bud. John had no idea that his previous efforts to clear them out would lead to so many following the noise here. I told John to stay put and I un-barricaded the back door, stepped through and jumped my fence, avoiding the glass by throwing over an old bath towel.

Taking careful aim with my weapon I started aiming for the nearest ones first or the ones on the outside of the circle, thinking that this may slow their pursuit down as they trip over their slain. I only had four magazines, that is 116 rounds. I shot round after round into the skulls of those things. One would think that it would bring instant death. This was not the case. Even some direct hits didn't hit the brain, but skirted along the outside of the skull only to pass through on the other side. For every ten I shot, I only killed eight or nine.

The lumbering mass of ghouls chased me as I tripped over the corpse-laden ground. I had no choice. I had to flee. I ran for blocks only to find more of them. I knew this was a dead place. I could feel it in the air and the vibrations of their moans hit my chest like a cheap band in a local nightclub. I was being hunted. The nearest immediate shelter I could find was a gas station. My body was full of adrenaline. I knew they would consume me if I gave quarter.

I climbed a pipe on the side of the gas station wall and stood flat-footed on the roof. I could tell by the moans and movement in the distance that I was a dead man and lived on borrowed time. I had around thirty rounds left (one magazine and some change). So I decided to take one out of the magazine, and save it for myself.

I started shooting. Trying for headshots. Hitting some and missing more, the fog of war was taking my aim or maybe it was the depression I was feeling, probably similar to someone that just found out they were HIV positive.

That is when I heard my savior. I caught glimpse of a car coming from the direction of my street. I kept shooting. The car took notice and headed my direction. It was John. He haphazardly pulled his car around the side of the gas station. There were five of them closing in. I took three of them out before I ran out of rounds. I had to go for my sidearm. I quickly jumped down from the roof, walked up and killed the last two at point blank, executioner style. A dark brown mist permeated the air behind their skulls. I stayed clear of it fearing infection and jumped in the car with John. We skipped shaking hands and John asked me if I wanted to go home. I told him that if we went back there, it would only lead them to us. He agreed. That was when I came up with the plan. I asked John if he could part with his car. John smiled and said, "What's your plan, sailor?"

I told John to keep driving. Those things were following us. I navigated him to a place not far from our homes. I asked John what type of music he had in his car. He was a conservative man. Looking through his CDs, I found what I was looking for. It would be perfect for the job. We made it to the place—a large parking lot next to a run down factory. We parked the car and I told John to keep it running. I put a CD in, rolled the windows down and opened all the doors. I turned everything on, even the wipers. Then I turned the volume up as loud as it would go without blowing the speakers. John and I grabbed our weapons and headed to a safer rally point a quarter of a mile away from his car.

The Marriage of Figaro was filling the air of the parking lot and surrounding area. The mass of the undead finally rounded the last corner and came into plain view of the car. Their shambling pace quickened as they saw what their glazed white eyes wanted them to see. They surrounded the car, and took it over. John and I wasted no more time. Once we saw that our plan worked, we headed out.

On the way home, I told John that I wasn't sure that even they could survive that music. He laughed and we kept moving. We saw a dozen of those things as we made our stealthy way back. None of them detected us. A half a bottle of whiskey later, here I sit. Staring at the bullet I saved for myself... —Is life worth living?

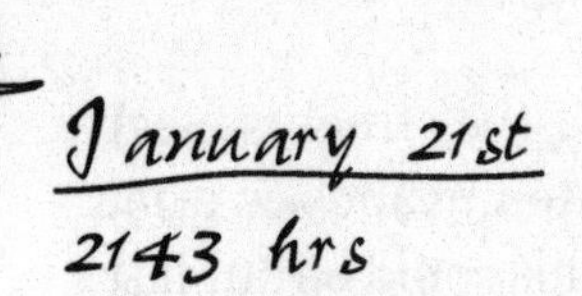

I have re-gathered my thoughts and recovered from yesterday's catastrophe and this morning's hangover. John and I have decided that it's better we stay in separate houses because it's "never good to put all of your eggs in one basket." We don't want both of us dying because one house is under siege. The events that transpired yesterday really hit me hard. I almost died out there. If John hadn't found me or had chosen not to, I would have spent days up there dying of dehydration, listening to the moaning of the dead, until I decided to end it.

There must have been five-hundred dead swarming the car when John and I left it there in the parking lot. Last night lying in my bed, I could hear the faint sound of Mozart in the distance when the wind blew just right. I can't hear it now. I can only imagine how long it took for the car to run out of gas on idle, and the battery to drain from everything that I had left on. The streets are clear now, but there is no way to know for how long. When the sound stopped drawing them near the car, I am sure they spread out again. It's only a matter of time until the law of averages puts them back here.

John and I talked. Last night before we left each other to our solitude (after the Figaro incident), John ran inside and handed me a few more packages of batteries for the 2-way radio. I could tell he wanted to talk. It wasn't until today that I got around to it. John knew I was messed up. Today I got to know him a little better. John is an engineer (explains his wacky plan with the yoga band). He has a Master's in mechanical engineering from Purdue. Told me that he worked for Execu-Tech.

He expressed his guilt about his son's probable fate, and that he felt like he pressured his son to go to the same college as good ole' dad. I told John that it really wouldn't matter where in the world he was when this happened. Apparently, it's just as bad everywhere.

After the debacle that I witnessed yesterday, I know that not many would or could survive this. I'm down to 884 rounds of .223 ammunition. I think that anything below 500 is critically low considering that they probably out number me thousands to one. Maybe even more. This can't be a battle of attrition, as a pyrrhic victory is not an option.

John and I are meeting tomorrow, providing the street is clear enough. We are going to discuss an exploration attempt and see what type of supplies we can gather. It's quite possible this could be our last few days here. I firmly believe that the government has collapsed. We basically canned the oilrig idea, as it would put us through countless miles of terrain ruled by the dead. When/if we bug out, it's going to have to be both a realistic plan and defensible location.

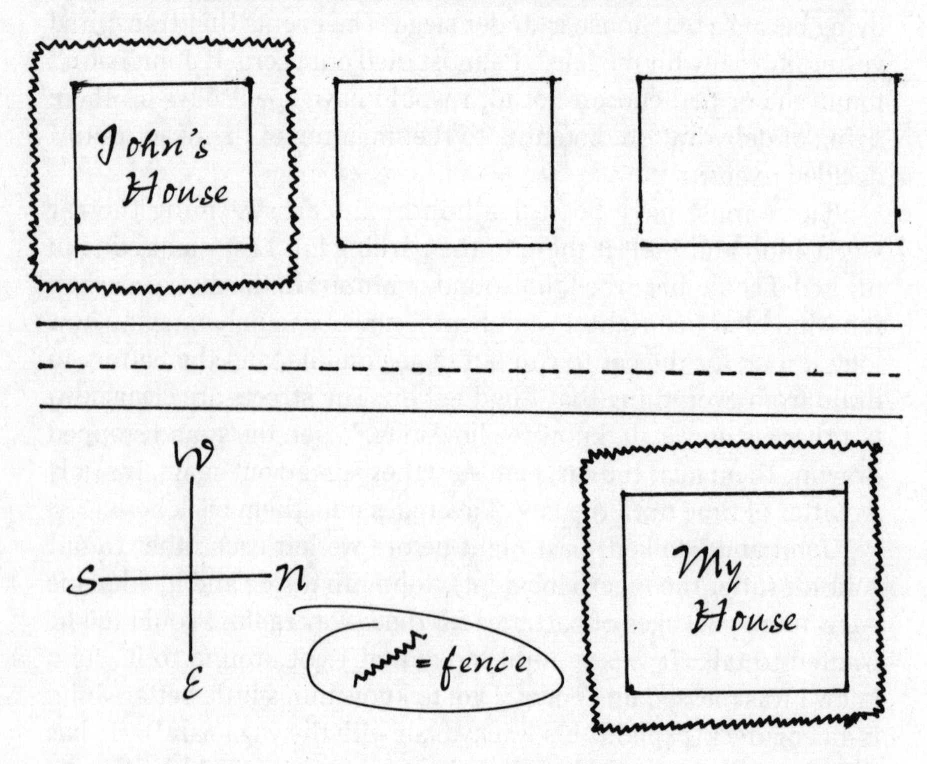

It would be impossible to close off the neighborhood with those things running around. The only thing I could think of would be to somehow drive a few tractor trailer rigs to each end of the street and use one to pull another trailer over on its side (to prevent them from crawling underneath). Then we could use smaller vehicles to fill in the gaps. This plan is lunacy. Before we even put one semi truck into place the street would be swarming with them. What I wouldn't give for a seaplane with a full tank of juice right now. I wonder how my base is holding up. I bet the gates are still holding. Worst case, the large planes (737s) carried survivors to a safe place long before they got in. I need time to brainstorm. Goodnight journal.

January 22nd

2240 hrs

John is here now. We decided it best to plan in person rather than try to coordinate this effort over the 2-way. He is in the kitchen feeding his dog. John and I are going to attempt to locate an aircraft suitable for flight. We spent the day packing our essentials, and we are going to head out at first light. John is going to leave his dog in the basement with enough food and water for five days. The bonus is she can't be heard if she decides to bark while she is in the basement. I feel sorry for her but this is no world for man's best friend. While I'm out, I'm going to attempt to locate more weapons.

One thing of particular interest that I will be bringing is a car battery jump kit. My car just isn't going to cut it. The plan is to leave in the morning in my car, (since John's car is useless to us now) and immediately look for alternate transportation. Any type of military vehicle would be best. An armored car would be optimal, but the chance of that happening is about the same as monkeys flying out of my ass. I am wondering if the GPS satellites are still functioning without human intervention. If we do happen to find an aircraft, I wouldn't mind having GPS as a back up navigation tool. I plan to keep writing in my journal while I am away. I think that we will be back in three days, nothing further than three hundred miles. We plan on heading to a location near the outskirts of Austin, TX. We won't be going into the city, especially after my fiasco at the convenience store a couple days ago. I still start shaking and smelling gunpowder and sweat when I think of that.

January 23rd

0600 hrs

John and I are off. Change of plans...back in two days not three.

1000 hrs

We departed this morning at around 0600. We are currently in Universal City. I packed my car while it was in the garage to avoid any unwanted guests then turned the ignition over, it sputtered but started. There is not much room in the Volvo, so our first mission was to find suitable transportation. We made it to the 1604 loop. I have never seen so much chaos. The road was littered with abandoned vehicles. I used my binoculars to survey the area. Panning the binoculars left to right, what I saw was disturbing. Reminded me of the traffic camera I saw before (seems like weeks ago). Some of those things were trapped inside with seat belts on. It looked like some left their windows down and were attacked and left to re-animate. We found what we were looking for, although the color wasn't ideal.

A canary yellow Hummer H2 was sitting cross ways on the loop with the driver's side door open. John and I parked the car out of view, took our weapons and car jump kit, and slowly skirted the knoll near the edge of the 1604 loop. The only movement we could see were a few of them walking around a good distance away and of course the movement of those trapped in the vehicles.

As we neared the H2, I saw something that I will never forget. A car seat strapped in the back. I told John to stay put while I approached. I didn't want him to see this, since I know he is or was a father.

I opened the back door of the vehicle. There it was, a shell of a human infant, writhing in the seat reaching for me. The black circles around its eyes looked like orbs. I wanted to cry as I unfastened the seat and set it on the ground a safe distance away. Just as I sat the car seat down and bent back up, I saw her. A woman badly disfigured wearing a pear of jeans and a t-shirt and boots was slowly moving about not more than a few meters up the road.

She caught glimpse of me and started walking toward me. A high shrill moan escaped her decomposing frame. I desperately tried to figure out a way to quietly dispose of her. I knew we were going to have to jump the Hummer (causing noise) because the driver side door had probably been open for days, if not weeks, leaving the dome light on.

She approached slowly and steadily. I looked inside the Hummer. There was a pillow in the passenger seat. I quickly grabbed the pillow, took off my belt and wrapped the pillow around the muzzle of my CAR-15, fastening it tightly with the belt. She was on me so I had no choice but to fire. Just as her gnarling lips curled over her yellow teeth, I pulled the trigger on my carbine.

The weapon made no more noise than popping popcorn as the monster's head exploded in a dark mist behind her. She was no more. I knelt down to the small infant. I sat there and meditated over what had to be done. I prayed that if there were a god, I would be forgiven. I dispatched the young one with my knife. No further details about that need to be given.

After the previous encounter, I threw the pillowcase over the car seat and signaled John to come over. I didn't see any immediate threat in the area, sans one of them in a car twenty feet away thrashing about. John brought the portable jumper (basically a charged battery with cables to connect to dead battery). I unfastened the hood restraints, leaned in the driver's door and popped the hood and went back into the car to check for keys. No keys. I sat there and reasoned for a minute.

What happened to the driver of this vehicle? Would he/she be so selfish as to leave their infant to die here at the whim of those things? After careful thought, I realized that maybe the parents didn't leave the infant. Checking the interior of the vehicle, I noticed a pink pine tree air freshener hanging from the rearview mirror. I then looked down on the ground at the ghoul thing that I had just killed. I checked her pockets and found the keys to the H2 as well as her driver's license. Sorry about your baby Ms. Rogers.

I took the keys and tried to turn over the ignition, just as I thought. Dead. I took the portable jumper and hooked it up while John turned the key. She roared to life. Checked the gas. It was running off fumes. John jumped in the passenger seat and we were off. We did sort of a u-turn and drove back in the direction of my car. On the way up the embankment, I looked in the rear view and I could tell instantly that we had gained some unwanted attention. I would guess a score of them were lumbering toward our vehicle about three hundred yards off. I stopped the Hummer next to my car and quickly loaded the supplies into the back of our new vehicle. We then headed to the nearest location that we could get fuel. John and I knew that the pumps would not work without electricity, so we brought part of a garden hose to siphon the gasoline.

After about two miles of driving and weaving in an out of wrecked traffic, I spotted a side road and took it. We drove for a half a mile before we found a car that was old enough to probably not have a anti-siphoning screen. Its hazard lights were blinking dimly, probably been flashing for weeks. We checked the perimeter and didn't see any threat. I parked the H2 in a position that would make siphoning easier. We drained every drop from the car, but this only put us at half a tank. It would have to do as the gas stations are all closed.

Blue Light Special, Aisle 13

2243 hrs

If there was hell on earth, I found it today. I am thinking about just throwing my camera away, as I don't think anyone would ever want to see these images even if mankind somehow survived this ordeal. All I see are images of death and destruction.

I drove most of the way. After we left Universal city, we headed up I-35 toward San Marcos, dodging in and out of cars and those fucking puss sacks. It is taking its toll on me. I have a new found respect for combat veterans that saw death every day. I don't see how they did it. I could see the smoke over Austin well before we even got to San Marcos. We needed gas, so I took exit 190 and veered off, taking a right into a long abandoned Wal-Mart parking lot.

John kept a lookout while I relieved myself in the ditch. I did the same for him. We pulled the Hummer near some cars so we could siphon more needed gas. At least this time we found a late 80's model Chevy Blazer that had a full tank. We filled the Hummer up to over 3/4 full. I was sitting somewhere around 880 rounds of .223 and 300 rounds of 9mm. John had two bricks of .22. I approached John and asked him if he felt like doing a little shopping.

The door was locked when we got to the front. I went back to the Hummer to pull it up front and check the tool kit for a pry bar. I found what I was looking for and commenced to try and pry the door from its lock. I got good leverage and put my back into it. John was watching the parking lot to make sure we didn't have any surprises. I kept tugging. All of the sudden I felt a thud on the door. I looked up and much to my chagrin; there he was... —A corpse in a bloody blue Wal-Mart vest pawing at the glass door drying to get out. The thing walked right into the door and bumped into the door latch on the inside.

The door came open slightly as the thing tried to ease itself out to us. It poked its head out and I took that opportunity to drive my tire tool into its head through the eye socket, killing it instantly. I held the door open like a gentleman and let the corpse fall out onto the sidewalk. I opened the door fully and placed the trashcan there to keep it open.

I told John that I thought that there were probably more inside. We pulled the Hummer so close to the entrance that no one could get in, and no one could get out unless they went in the driver's side door and climbed out the passenger door. It was my idea in the event some visitors decided to show up during our shopping spree. I showed John how to handle his weapon inside closed quarters conditions. I call it the recon glide as I had picked it up from one of my marine friends. John and I eased through the aisles...goddamn it...why does Wal-Mart always have to put sporting goods in the back?

I motioned to John to look where I was looking. It was another worker that must have been killed during a shift. It slowly walked toward us. I gave John the signal to shoot, because his weapon is much quieter than mine. With a careful aim, John took the creature out and it lay lifeless on the floor.

Thank god for the skylights because without them, this idea could kiss my ass. John and I continued to the back. We made it to sporting goods and found that many of the guns were either sold out or looted. There were many boxes of .223 ammo and also many boxes of twelve gauge shells. There was one gun of particular interest left in the cases; —A Remington 870 twelve gauge pump. I saw fit to break the glass and give it to John since he was lacking in the firepower department. We took the shells and rounds for the carbine, and started to make our escape.

John and I were constantly scanning the aisles for ghouls. Just as I rounded the corner from sporting goods, I was pulled off my feet by a female corpse. I hit the ground hard and felt a tug at my ankle. I felt a hard pinch as the thing tried to bite me through the heel of my combat boots. I gave her a hard kick to the nose and heard the cartilage snap as I hit home. I got up and stepped back, checking my heel for wounds. Thank goodness for Altama boots. She didn't get up, as her back had been broken by a large shelf that had fallen on her probably weeks before. She snarled at me. John took aim...I signaled him not to shoot. I walked up to her and brought my heel down on her temple as hard as I could. She was no longer a factor.

We made it to the front and just as I thought, a welcoming committee was there to greet us. I stood and counted thirty of them. John climbed through the window over the driver's seat and I did the same and sat driver. I started the ignition and rolled up my window. We would have been in a pickle if we hadn't wedged the H2 inches from the open door to the store. As we pulled out into the parking lot, I lost all care and just mowed them over. John was busy pulling the stickers and tags off his new Remington.

It was time to find shelter, as the sun was starting to get low. We got on the service road along I-35 north and started to look for a spot to stay. I recommended to John that we find a semi-safe spot and just sleep in the Hummer. He agreed and joked, "The motel six isn't exactly open anyway."

I kept driving, until we reached a small town called "Kyle" just south of Austin. There was a sign that read; —Kyle, Texas "Welcome Home." That was when I noticed the spot. There was a large hay field with a fence around it and no sign of any of those things shambling around. I pulled into the drive and picked up the t-handle that held the gate in place. Motioned John to switch seats and pull through so I could secure the gate again. We pulled the Hummer in between four round bails of hay. The bails covered up the sides of the vehicle so that if anything approached, it would have to do so from the front or the back. John and I made sure all doors were locked, and John went to sleep. It's 2330 now, so I suppose I should do the same.

January 24th

1534 hrs

John and I awoke at 0615 this morning to the sound of a rooster crow in the distance. I started the H2 up and pulled out from between the hay. We pulled over to the gate, and looked down the road from the direction that we came. There were a lot of them in the distance. Couldn't tell if they were heading our way. Could it be possible that they heard our vehicle and were following the sound this far? I hope not.

We arrived at the outskirts of Austin, TX at 0705. The smoke was almost unbearable. Visibility was only at around a hundred yards. Every now and again when the wind would blow just right, I could catch a glimpse of the taller buildings in the distance. One of them looked like a torch, as its tip was burning brightly. To the right I could see what looked like an airport air traffic control tower. John and I took the next road to the right toward the tower.

We made it to the outer perimeter fence. It was a small private airport with a few Cessna aircraft and two small jets sitting inside open hangars. A section of the fence was destroyed so we drove right up onto the tarmac. We surveyed the area and didn't see any immediate danger. I tied off a rope to the front nose wheel of one of the Cessna 172 (picked out the best looking one) and opened the cockpit door. To my surprise, sitting in the passenger seat, I found the aircraft pilot's kneeboard, flight computer and chart.

I climbed in the cockpit and yelled at John to take it slow and easy and to pull us over to the refueling station. I shut the door and concentrated on the checklist so that I could turn the aircrafts electrical system on and check the gauges for fuel or anything out of the ordinary. Every few seconds I felt the aircraft tug, as John towed the aircraft and I to the pumps. After checking the gauges, I was happy to find that both wing tanks were full, so I opened up the door, jumped out and ran ahead to tell John to flip a bitch and pull the bird back to the tower.

At the tower I used the aircraft checklist to do a walk around inspection. I didn't fancy the idea of losing my engine over a heavily infested area. I prepped the bird for flight and discussed with John our next plan of action. We took out our atlas and looked for the nearest airport to our homes back in San Antonio. I looked and looked and all I could find was the international airport in the center of the city. That was unacceptable.

John bent down and had a puzzled look on his face. He asked me if I had ever been to the "Retama Park Racetrack" off of I-35. He told me we passed it on our way out of town. I had never heard of it since I hadn't lived there long. John asked how much length I needed to land the plane. I went out to the cockpit and looked in the chart compartment. I couldn't find any info. Some of the smaller planes I have flown needed maybe 1,000 ft if I used beta. This bird didn't have beta controls. I had to take a guess. I would probably need 1,500 ft minimum. John said that he thought it might work.

John and I brought our weapons up and carefully approached the tower entry doors. John opened the door and I took point. The elevator was obviously out so we had to take the stairs. We shut and latched the door behind us as we quietly ascended. There were windows at the top of every flight overlooking the runway. I heard and saw nothing until we got to the top of the stairs. I saw a coagulated pool of blood sitting in front of the tower control center door.

I motioned for John to look. I walked up to the door, slowly opened it, and jumped in ready to blast. I didn't expect to see this... One of the controllers had taken out four of those things and then probably out of despair had turned his pistol on himself and did the same. I opened up the doors to the observation deck and John and I threw the bodies over the side, opposite the side the aircraft was on.

John and I went back down stairs to unload the H2. We brought everything into the tower just to be careful. I locked up the Hummer and went upstairs to plan.

John expressed to me that he would not leave his dog in the basement to starve to death. I understood. John told me that he would take the H2 and meet me at the racetrack and then we would both go to the house in the H2 together. I would have to fly the bird and land safely at the track. I had many hours in military aircraft, but never in a Cessna. It was going to be risky, but necessary.

I calculated that it would only take me around 35 minutes to do the startup checklist get airborne and be over the track. This meant that in order to conserve fuel, John was going to have to leave before I did. It was a two-hour trip for him. I showed John my calculations and he agreed it would be best he leave first.

2243 hrs

Dark outside. Only fires can be seen in the distance. Found some airport departure/approach plates for this airstrip. It was a good thing too. Because of the documents, I found out that there is a water tower two hundred feet high off the departure end of the runway. I would never have seen it in time with all the smoke. Now at least I know what general direction to fly when I get off the ground. It's time for sleep now.

January 25th

0700 hrs

It was time to fly the coop, literally. John and I went outside this morning and looked down at the base of the tower. Apparently we had made too much noise. There were ten of them walking around the tower, bumping into it, making metal tapping sounds. I distracted them as John threw the non-breakable supplies to the ground so that we would not have to make multiple trips. John came over to me and handed me his .22. I told him I would take care of them while he consolidated the supplies. Visibility was still only around 100 yards.

I shot the creatures and quickly helped John with the last of the supplies. We made it down the stairs without incident. I took what I needed for the flight, i.e. my guns, some food and water, and left John with the rest. I asked John if he were sure. He said yes. I told him I would meet him at the track at 0930 hours. Last night we took a portable radio from the tower, so John could reach me on 121.5 when we needed to talk. It was the aviation distress frequency. Doubt anyone would mind.

John got in the Hummer and drove off. I got in the aircraft, and locked the doors, and started checking everything I could for the wait. All the smoke in the air and poor visibility must be fucking their senses up. I figured that those gunshots would have attracted more. I am getting scared, and am leaving now...

0812 hrs

I'm in the air now. The aircraft is trimmed up (so I can go hands free) and I am headed back to the track. Decided to do a little recon mission since I was in the air so early. This plane is relatively easy to fly. I thought it would be more trouble than this. After taking off, I decided to head toward the base and see if the walls were still intact. I remembered the VOR frequency, dialed it in to the navigation aid and followed the needle. My heart sank as I descended through the clouds at 2,000 feet.

I flew right over the base, as low as I could and saw the horror. Every building was either on fire, or destroyed... —Looked like an air strike. That might explain what happened to Austin, TX. I pulled the aircraft around into a shallow fifteen-degree angle of bank and headed toward the gate. The gate was totally destroyed, and through the smoke, I could see thousands of walking dead dominating the landscape inside the base. I then brought the bird on general course to make rendezvous the track.

2356 hrs

I am home.
Don't feel like writing.
The dead are the lucky ones.

Hindsight is 20/20

January 26th
1842 hrs

Yesterday was a hard day. I made it to the track with plenty of fuel to spare. The fence was intact and there were no creatures present. Looked like I was going to have enough room to land, but noticed that the track was uneven and it looked like about a ten-degree grade. I was going to have to show some good aileron control to keep both wheels solid when I landed.

I came over the northern end of the track at 85 knots. Pulled back power, flared, touched the back two wheels...eased the elevator control and brought the nose down. Pulled power back to idle, and let her roll to a stop (no breaks, since the track was dirt). Looked down at my kneeboard and flipped the pages to the engine shutdown checklist, I shut her down after I taxied her to a less visible spot on the back end of the track.

Now came the waiting game. It was 0930 when I set down. I didn't see the H2 anywhere, and it would be difficult to miss a canary yellow H2 even at two miles visibility. If John came, he would see the bird, and know I was near. I decided to try and find something to cover the plane up with so it would be less noticeable to anyone... living or dead. This was a racetrack, so I was sure there is some type of tarp somewhere. I took my rifle and headed for the maintenance area. Outside the chain link fence of the track, there were numerous undead walking around. Some of them were rapping on the fence, angry at their inability to walk through it. I know that if enough of them came, they would do just that.

I approached the maintenance area with caution. I stood in front of the steel door and listened...I could hear the sound of banging metal. Sounded like someone was using a hammer on the floor inside...My philosophy has always been stealth over confrontation. I walked around the building looking for windows. I found one in the rear, about eight feet off the ground. The only problem was that there was a corpse shambling about on the opposite side of the fence. It couldn't get to me, but I concluded that it would make a lot of noise if it saw me. Window was a "no go." I quietly hugged the wall back to the door.

The sound had stopped. This was really fucking with my head. I couldn't take it anymore so I eased the door open and looked inside. It was dark, except for the spear of light shining in through the window that I had seen. I could smell rotting flesh.

I shut the door again. My instincts told me, fuck the plane cover; it's not that important. For some reason I ignored that completely logical thought process. I took out my LED light and tightened it on the light mount of my rifle. I switched the light on and opened the door again. Put the muzzle of my weapon in so that I could light up the dark garage. The smell was almost unbearable.

The source of the noise became immediately apparent. A dead mechanic, crushed by a hydraulic lift was lying there on his back, reanimated, and banging a torque wrench on the ground. A low grunt came from his badly mutilated body as he tried to look up at me. He was reaching for me. It was then, all in the span of a second that the following happened:

I saw the bite marks of the flesh that had been torn away on his face and neck. I knew that he didn't do it to himself, and deduced that there was another dead fucking corpse in the room. Last but not least, the door flew open and I was tackled by one of them (best guess, the same one that had the mechanic for lunch).

The only thing that was keeping this stink ridden shit ball from biting my nose off was the fact that I had my weapon wedged between us. I pushed it off, and it (couldn't tell male or female) grabbed my wrist. I gave it a nice rifle butt to the head and it fell back. I immediately got to my feet and popped a round in its miserable head. I wanted to just fucking mow it in half, but the reasonable half of me kicked in and I told myself not to waste the ammunition.

The door to the garage was shut, and it was going to fucking stay that way. I could hear the sound of fists on the door, and I knew that there were more inside. I went back on the side of the garage where I saw some oil drums and rolled one of them back around to the front, to put in the doorway and prevent whatever was behind that door from opening it and ruining my day.

No more exploring. I carefully started walking back toward the plane. I noticed that I had gathered an entourage of fans on the other side of the fence. I guess they enjoyed my little execution. They were gnashing their teeth on the metal wire and groaning and beating on the chain link fence. Watching this motley crew of gray evil made me very uneasy.

About that time, I heard a vehicle approaching. I hid behind one of the concession stands and watched. The ugly yellow confirmed my suspicions. It was John. I ran up to the gate to let him in. It was locked.

Reluctantly, I pulled the carbine up to fire, aiming for the part that touched the chain and not the actual lock...Three rounds and the lock fell off the chain. I was thinking to myself that shooting locks only worked in movies as I yanked the chain off and pulled the gate open. John came screaming through. I quickly shut the gate, wrapped the chain back around the gate and ran over to the aircraft. I remembered seeing a c-clamp in the cockpit clamped to a headset. I quickly unscrewed it and ran back toward the gate. There were a few of them already within a rock throw. I put the c-clamp through both ends of the chain and tightened it down. Wouldn't stop a living person, but I doubt these miserable shells of human beings could figure it out.

I walked back over to the plane where John was parked. I looked at him. His cheek was bleeding. I asked him what happened. He told me that he had to make a stop to siphon some gas and ended up having to shoot three of those dead people. He killed the first one and on the second shot, he missed and the round ricocheted off a concrete embankment, hitting him in the cheek. He killed the last one and got the fuck out of there. Luckily he was finishing up the siphoning when this happened.

When I first saw him, I thought he had been bitten or scratched and my only friend in the world was going to be one of "them."

I told John that I probably had about two hours worth of fuel left, (roughly 190 nautical miles at max cruise speed of 95 knots).

The plane was ready to fly. John and I decided it best to leave the plane and head home to figure things out from there. We were only maybe a twenty-minute drive from home. I collected my things out of the plane and put them in the Hummer. We were going to have to distract those things if were going to get back out the way John drove in.

I walked over to the gate, and got their attention. I used myself as bait (they were on the other side of the fence) and lured them to follow me while John got ready to make the escape in the Hummer. They followed me to the other end of the fence. This gave me two hundred yards to sprint back, open the gate, get in, drive through, get out and shut the gate back. No problem. It went exactly like that. John and I drove toward our home, dodging, surviving.

This was becoming second nature. John took a back street when we got to my neighborhood, and parked the vehicle in an empty building lot. We took our weapons, and essentials, and made like shadows back to John's. We avoided being seen by few of those things along the way. We jumped John's wall, and he rushed in to check on his dog, and I secured the rest of the house. His dog came running upstairs, jumping up on John and licking his face. I told John that since I had power we should use my house as a base. After all, if were going to die, might as well be together. It's funny how attitudes change.

Today, we spent moving John's gear over here, one trip at a time, avoiding being seen. I had a feeling we would be taking to the air sometime in the nearer future.

January 27th

1713 hrs

I'm glad John is an engineer. He thought of a way to make an alarm device that could save us in a pinch. We thought of it today when we had to go out and quietly put down one of <u>them</u> that was beating loudly on my back gate. I killed it with an ice pick taped to a metal pipe with duct tape. It was then that John asked me what I thought of his plan. He wanted to wire a battery-powered radio to the mailbox of a house two doors down. He said that he had quite a bit of wire in his basement and that it would work. We slipped over to his house to gather some supplies and the wire. His basement was full of Annabelle dung.

He took his battery powered alarm clock radio and the wire, and a simple light switch (that we cannibalized from his house), and made a sort of remote alarm. Our thinking was that if those things got the jump on us in the night, and there were too many of them, we could flip the switch, turn on the radio and use the noise to draw them to the mail box across the street and a few doors down.

John wired it so that the radio/alarm would fit inside the mailbox, thus using the metal box as an amplifier. We tried it out for a second, and it was definitely loud enough, although we had to use the alarm function, as there were no more stations broadcasting. We wrapped the wire around the pillar of the box, and tucked it along the curb out of sight. The problem came when we had to get it across the street and into my wall for easy access. We brought the wire across the street and john and I took shovels and piled dirt over it so that those things would have a hard time tripping over it and yanking the connection loose. All in all, it was over 100 yards of wire.

I mounted the light switch for the alarm to a junction box using a kitchen magnet.

I will be spending most of the night figuring out where to go next. We might end up staying here for a while, but then again, the mood I was in yesterday might take over.

After our little invention was complete, I used my binoculars to check on the Hummer. From my vantage point, I could only see from the side view mirrors to the front. I could see 3-4 of them curiously wandering around it. I made sure to take a mental note of this.

January 28th
2039 hrs

While monitoring the citizen band today, I made a startling discovery. I intercepted a recording being transmitted out on CB channel nine for survivor volunteers to be members of the "new military." The broadcast was a recorded loop dated yesterday. The recording was calling for responses at the top of every hour. Something didn't sound right. If this was a band of left over military and they were calling out for replacements, what happened to the original members? Slain? Executed? No chances. I turned it off until about ten minutes shy of 1800 hours. I then listened in for any others out there that might volunteer.

"**static**, Shane Stahl here, Concord, Texas. Anyone there?"

"Yes, this is Captain Thomas Beverly formerly of the 24th special tactics squadron, it's good to hear your voice."

The conversation went on, and the two exchanged information and decided upon an extraction point not far from "Shane's" house, near a water tower off the interstate. John and I discussed this new development, and decided it best to continue monitoring and gathering information, until it could be discerned that this rogue group was in fact a benign group of left over volunteers.

Spent much of this morning reading over the aircraft manuals and emergency procedures. I wanted to be knowledgeable of this aircraft's systems the next time I took her up, just in case.

John and I discussed numerous destinations for our next outing. We had one of two options. Continue to stay here, and hope we don't get overrun, or take the bird and what we can fit inside and head southeast to the islands off the coast of Corpus Christi. There is a Naval air station in Corpus, and I'm sure there is plenty of fuel, and maybe even a better aircraft.

If we chose the bug out option, careful consideration would have to be given as to what equipment stays and what goes with us in the plane. John and I have a combined weight of 360 lbs. Add fuel and luggage to that, and we can only afford to fly with four hundred pounds of supplies. That was also pushing it, and that wasn't much when you added it all up. We began to make a list of things we absolutely could not leave. John listed, "dog, 20 lbs." I told John, not to worry, Annabelle was coming with us.

We wouldn't be leaving today, or tomorrow for that matter. I told John that I did not wish to die on my birthday.

January 29th

1250 hrs

A group of bikers came roaring through our neighborhood thirty minutes ago. John had to put the muzzle on Annabelle to keep her from barking. I doubt they would hear the bark over the roar of their engines, but my motto is "no chances." I counted 70-80 bikes as the convoy rolled past. Many bikes had passengers. Most bikes had long rifle/shotgun holsters mounted on them complete with weapon.

I noticed something that I don't think you would have seen before this epidemic. There weren't just cruisers, there were also racing bikes (crotch rockets) in the convoy. I bet they used the racers as recon scouts. Again this group looked rough and I didn't see it necessary to alert them of our presence.

1847 hrs

The sound of moaning, shuffling dead is almost unbearable. Three hours after the bike convoy came through, the creatures that were no doubt following them began their slow parade into the neighborhood. John and I are maintaining our silence. In the fading light there are too many of them to count. This could easily turn into the worst-case scenario. I do not think that they are alerted to our presence, but I cannot be sure. I can see them periodically looking in this direction, and walking into my wall, but I do not know if they are trying to get in, because of the noise.

I went to my gun cabinet and pulled out two sets of yellow foam earplugs and handed one to John. I told John that if we had to make a break for it tomorrow, we were going to need our rest. John stuck them in his pocket and nodded.

2213 hrs

We got our things ready just in case we had to make the great escape. Many of the ghouls have continued on their path in the direction of the bikers. Many more undead are seemingly lost and confused and have camped out here on our street, just walking around bumping each other and changing directions. It reminds me of my college physics class years ago. The molecules were bumping into each other in unpredictable patterns and just milling about on the slide. I would say a safe estimate puts the count at 85 walking dead. I can only go off the moon and starlight for my estimations.

Note to self: Find some NVGs most ricky-tick.

If today were a normal day, my fellow squadron officers and I would be getting shit faced at a random bar on the river walk. It was my birthday and I know they wouldn't allow me to stay inside like this. Well, I guess the celebration would have to wait. I had a shot of whiskey with John and toasted to survival. Goodnight.

Proverbial Beans

January 30th
1534 hrs

Bad news. While monitoring the television, and radio, John and I came across the first government broadcast in weeks. It was being transmitted over every available TV channel as well as over the AM bands. I think this might be because AM carries further than FM. It was the First Lady. In a solemn voice she relayed to what was left of the United States that the President had perished in an undead attack and died a week earlier. The armed forces were now in the control of the Vice President. She went on to say that the VP was in a secure location and that she hoped the best for America and the world.

She warned of rogue military factions that had deserted over the past weeks, and hoped that they would come to their senses and return to fight for their fallen Commander-In-Chief.

She saved the best for last.

She asked that anyone able to hear the following announcement, to do their best to spread the word, as she was sure that not many survivors had electricity, or access to a TV or radio.

She then spilled the proverbial beans.

"The President has authorized the use of tactical nuclear warheads on all major cities. On February the first at approximately 10:00 AM Central Standard Time, a strike force consisting of Joint Navy/Air force bombers will deploy high yield tactical nuclear warheads on major urban centers. We believe that this retaliation strike will give us the advantage we so desperately need to take back our country and eventually our world. The use of our Global Hawk and Predator UAV drones has revealed major populations of the undead in and around the targeted cities. If you are able to travel, and can hear this message, I urge you to make preparations to evacuate. We will now broadcast the list of designated target areas. Please look closely at the bottom of the television screen."

I could now see tears rolling down her face.

Nope, she wasn't bullshitting. They were going to do it. I watched and crossed my fingers. I knew my city was the 8th largest in the United States. I didn't kid myself. As the "letter R" cities rolled by, John and I held our breath. There it was… —San Antonio. John and I have been designated as a nuclear target. I live eighteen miles from the Alamo. The Alamo is in the center of San Antonio. The blast radius would be at least twenty miles, depending on the warhead. I bet they weren't taking any chances, meaning the blast radius would probably be more like fifty miles.

The instant that thought crossed my mind; I watched as the doomed cities rolled by on the bottom of the screen, a precautionary tutorial was being displayed. "Minimum safe distance is 150 miles from ground zero." This would mean that the government is using their mountain buster nukes and are pulling all stops.

I looked over at John and said, "I think it is time we thought about leaving this place."

January 31st

2341 hrs

Situation is not improving. John and I loaded up the Hummer for our trip to the racetrack. We will be flying out tonight. The moon is out so visibility will be great for flying. The text on the emergency broadcast is warning survivors that bombers will be dropping electronic sound decoys in the center of the designated cities to draw the undead in so that they will maximize the effectiveness of the explosion. The warning also made sure to mention that this would cause much more activity within the dead ranks. The jets flew overhead today at around noon and dropped their payload. I know it must be loud if I can here it from this far. It is sort of a high-pitched, oscillating whine. Annabelle doesn't like it but she is getting used to it, despite her hackles being perpetually raised.

It's hard to believe January will be over in a few minutes. John and I had to use our "mailbox sound device" today while loading the H2. This was a couple hours after the military dropped the sound decoy. The things were coming out of the woodwork and many of them were milling around our street. We made four trips until the things destroyed John's noisy invention. One of them finally yanked it out of the mailbox and used it as a bludgeon, denting the mailbox top. We loaded everything up and it's almost time to leave. It's dark outside and I have turned the lights off so that when we leave, our natural night vision will be already adjusted. John and I will be flying east in our small aircraft. I have studied the manuals over and over. Not much else to do besides count down hours.

I think we may be a little overweight on the bird. Oh well. I will get her in the air. Ten hours until the end of the world.

February 1st
0430 hrs

Nuclear Winter

The three of us (including Annabelle) slipped out the back last night and made for the Hummer. Our eyes were adjusted. Apparently Annabelle's were also as she warned us of a ghoul lurking in the shadows. John told me he felt the hair stand up on her back (he was carrying her) and we could both hear her quiet barks through the muzzle. I dispatched the creature with an aluminum bat and continued on to our vehicle. There were a few lurking around behind the vehicle, but they were a safe distance away and we were able to make it inside. Even through the window we could hear the oscillating whine of sound decoys. The unearthly moans of the dead in the distance seamed to rise over even the decoys.

The drive to the racetrack was pretty much uneventful. I drove slowly and kept my headlights off. Other than the occasional thump, of one of those things off my fender, there was nothing. The moonlight showed me the way.

We pulled up to the chain link gate that led to the track. I turned on my headlights and the c-clamp was still there just as I left it. My rifle and me exited the Hummer and went over to the gate and unlatched the clamp. Although I didn't see any of them around, I could smell them and sense their presence in the distance.

After pulling the Hummer in, I reattached the c-clamp. A hundred yards off I could faintly see the outline of one of the undead. No matter. It would take at least a hundred of them to breach the fence.

John and I unloaded the Hummer and packed up the Cessna. I performed the preflight checklist and got her ready to take to the air. I got in the cockpit and performed the engine start checklist. She started with no difficulty. Checked the fuel pressure and quantity and it was all in the green. John and I both latched our exterior doors and I turned on my landing/takeoff lights. It was then that I had remembered my gruesome discovery a few days before, the poor mechanic that been crushed under a lift and dined upon.

I also remembered my encounter with one of them, and how I killed it and put a 55 gallon oil drum in front of the door to keep whatever else was in there from getting out.

My landing lights were pointing at the garage door. The door was wide open; the barrel was tipped over on its side. It was at that time the garage's mystery resident showed itself. A loud thump on the pilots side window and then the thing was there...drooling and pressing its lips to the cockpit glass like one of those algae suckers in a fish tank. It scared the shit out of me. I can't believe I forgot about the garage until I was in the plane. That could have been my demise. I started to taxi to my takeoff area; —The thing was shuffling after the plane. I tried to avoid hitting it with my propeller, as I didn't want to risk any damage.

I pushed the throttle to full power, and fed a rich mixture of fuel to the engine. We started to lurch forward. My anti-collision strobes were making the stadium look like it was in a thunderstorm. I looked in my rear view mirror and could see two ghouls inside the perimeter shuffling toward me.

50 knots...60 knots...75 knots...I pulled the controls back and started to climb. It was going to be close. The engine strained as I put her at max blast. I could almost swear that I felt my main landing gear touch one of the bleachers as I cleared the top row of seats.

We were airborne, and flying SSE in the direction of Corpus. Earlier, before we left for the Hummer, John and I checked the TV/ Radio and checked it twice to make sure that there wasn't a nuke on its way there with our names on it. The same cities were scrolling across the bottom of the screen. I guess Corpus just wasn't big enough. Damn, I know they have enough nukes...but somehow I bet they were running low on pilots to drop them.

En route, we could make out the faint signs of headlights on the interstate. I wondered if it were other survivors evacuating. I could do no good and would probably get both John and I killed if we attempted to land on or near the interstate.

I was flying at 7,000 feet in accordance with Visual Flight Rules (VFR) out of habit. Somehow, I don't think an airborne collision is likely since I'm probably the only manned prop plane in the air in all of North America. I'm certain that there were probably several Predator drones patrolling the skies, giving status reports on the multiplying dead below.Half way to Corpus I saw something I didn't expect... —Lights, actual electric lights. Yes, fires were commonplace since we took off, but not electricity.

According to my charts we were approaching "Beeville, TX." There was a small municipal airstrip there. I checked my fuel, and knew it would be close, so John and I decided to buzz the airport, since it had lights and see if we could land safely. I was flying southeast above I-37 when I broke off for Beeville municipal airport. Miraculously, the GPS satellites were still working and I keyed the coordinates into the GPS (28-21.42N / 097-47.27W). The green LCD was pointing in the same direction that I was headed so I knew I was on course.

We arrived at the airstrip about eight minutes later, just like the GPS indicated and I lowered my altitude to 800 feet, to check the runways. The runways ran NW to SE. I decided to flyby runway 12, since the wind would favor my landing there. The directional beacons were still on, so I knew I could make the landing as long as there wasn't something parked on the tarmac. After one flyby, I brought her around for a landing. On my first pass, I saw a fuel truck sitting next to the taxiway.

I landed the plane, and taxied over to the fuel truck. I left the plane running and walked around the back toward the truck. My rifle was at the ready in case anything was to go wrong. I turned my LED light on and its bright beam illuminated the area around the truck. I forgot to turn off the anti-collision strobes when I got out of the plane, so they were flashing brightly, giving me snapshots of the area every two seconds.

I walked over to the hose, pulled it off the rung and checked the pressure on the fuel pump. Looks like it was never shut off. No matter, it wouldn't drain the battery unless it was constantly pumping. There was enough fuel in this truck to fly cross-country two or three times. Too bad I couldn't take it all. I walked over and unlatched the fuel cap on the wing with a wood block that was inside the door. I didn't want to take any chances with spark. I normally wouldn't leave the engine running to refuel, but hey, I wasn't taking any chances of this bird not wanting to start. I filled the tanks up until some of it started splashing out on the wing. I returned the hose to its cradle on the fuel truck and started to walk back. I couldn't hear anything over the engines. As I walked back to the plane, John was frantically trying to signal me. He jumped out and started running toward me. I turned around and instinctively raised my weapon. Good timing.

I squeezed off a round and decapitated the creature from pretty much point blank...Glad I had John with me, because this seven-foot puss sack was the right height to bend down and just take a hunk out of my neck before I knew what hit me. The thing was just a convulsing maggot pie on the ground now. John shot me a worried glance and got back in the bird with Annabelle. She didn't like flying, and puked twice since we took off.

Got back into the air and continued for Corpus. Checking the chart, Corpus was 144 miles from San Antonio. We needed 150 miles safe distance. It was 0315 when we were back airborne. That meant 6 hrs and 45 minutes until they dropped their payload. An hour after taking off from Beeville, we were over Corpus airspace. Our destination would be the Naval Air Station east of the city. It would give us our minimum safe distance. Naval Air Station Corpus Christi is a training base. The aircraft there would be of no tactical importance, just single engine reliable training turboprops.

The lights were still on at the Naval base. They must be using an on site generator. Most bases have alternate sources of power in the event of enemy attack on the power grid. As I flew over the base, destruction was apparent. The base perimeter was destroyed and there were hundreds of them on the base. Same routine...checked the airfield. The tower beacon was still operational and flashing its white/blue signal.

The lights inside the tower were on and I could see no movement inside the airfield perimeter as I made my pass (there was a separate fence for the airfield and admin/tower buildings). I could see 50 or 60 single engine prop aircraft on the taxiways parked. T-34c Turbo mentors, and T-6 Texans made up the bulk of them. That was more like it. I was familiar with the T-34c, and I knew they all had parachutes (unlike the Cessna). John and I decided to land near the tower and use it as shelter for the night. We landed the plane and quickly shut the engine down near the tower as to avoid attracting too many of them. The door to the tower was unlocked but it was shut. Just as I suspected, the tower was abandoned. No sign of life or death inside. John and I took our food/water and weapon and ammo inside for the night, locking the door behind us. It was a heavy steel door and I knew it would hold.

Ground Zero

1050 hrs

John and I finally got to sleep around 0540 this morning. The tower was clean and quiet and safe, and that felt good. I set the alarm on my watch for 0930, to give me thirty minutes of prep time for the show. We turned on the radio; the same message was being looped from the other day. Around 1005 I knew it happened. The blast wave must have been traveling at immense speed. The wind picked up and I could see the trees blowing toward the east, not swaying. My eyes were trained northwest toward the direction of San Antonio. I saw it. It was small from this distance, but it was there.

We witnessed a bright orange mushroom cloud on the horizon. Damn, they must have really dropped the big one for me to see and feel the wind from over 150 miles. It was a clear, calm day. I knew the wind would not be radioactive from this distance, but the force that pushed the wind was. I just hope that the gas cloud didn't drift this way.

I noticed something else that was odd. Houston was northeast of me. John was checking that direction. There was no blast. Granted it was 217 miles away. Just odd. I wondered if they were running late.

The tower has electricity, water pressure and radios. I think I am going to stay here and ponder what just happened.

February 2nd

1435 hrs

I woke up this morning and grabbed the binoculars to survey the area. The first thing I checked was the windsock. It was blowing west. That was good news. I wouldn't be glowing in the dark today. The airfield was secure. All Naval air stations have eight-foot high chain link fences to keep unauthorized personnel off of the flight line. There were numerous dead around the perimeter in the distance. They were paying no attention to the fence; they were just there.

Annabelle was whining. John was monitoring the radios, so I decided to take her out (it was the "I have to pee" whine). Walked her down the stairs and took her out to a patch of grass on the side of the tower opposite the runways. She did her business and sniffed the air. She is a small dog, but she has a good sniffer. The hair on the back of her neck was standing up again. I took her back upstairs and shut the door to the tower behind me. The tower had a 360-degree view, so I walked around the center over to the grassy side to see maybe if I could catch a glimpse of what was pissing her off.

There was nothing. It is probably the wind carrying a bad smell to her. She was happy again, and I poured her some water and gave her some dog food. John was wearing headphones, listening. In the control towers everyone used headsets because it would be chaos if every radio played out loud. John was clearly listening to something besides static. I walked over to his panel, checked his frequency and went to another terminal to listen.

There were two pilots talking to each other. One of them asked the other if they had both made the best decision. They must have been near our tower, or we wouldn't pick them up. They probably thought they had all the privacy in the world right now. As far as they knew, no one was alive to listen to them in this area. I wondered what they meant. Were these the same pilots that dropped the nukes? My question was soon answered. As their conversation went on, I discovered that these pilots refused to drop their ordnance. They didn't see it as a good decision, so instead of following their orders, apparently they chose exile.

I really can't blame them. They were human, just like me. I am not sure I could have dropped it either. I wonder which cities were spared. My guess was that one of them was Houston, or maybe even Austin, although the San Antonio blast might have taken care of them.

John and I couldn't carry all of our food and water on the plane with us. Water wasn't a problem right now, but I would say in a couple weeks food would be. Last night the fire to the northwest was bright. Every thing that could burn was probably burning. I bet my house was nothing but dust now.

2143 hrs

After rummaging through the tower, John and I came across a large aluminum case with a master lock attached. We were able to pry it open with a set of bolt cutters from the maintenance closet one flight down. The case was a foam padded equipment case used to store night vision goggles. There were four sets inside, monocular type, using civilian AA batteries. I should have known. Tower controllers use them at night to warn pilots of obstructions on the runway. Most military airfield towers have them. Now John and I had them. They were shit for depth perception, but hey, I felt better with them.

I tried them out. John and I turned off all interior lights. I adjusted the focus and starlight power. The airfield was bathed in a green glow. These were going to be really useful. I could even see field mice scurrying on the runway, near the planes. Tomorrow, I'm going to go out and check the planes for myself.

February 3rd
1523 hrs

I went out this morning to check on a few of the aircraft and pick out the best one in case John and I had to leave. These turboprops were much more reliable than the Cessna, and I at least had some hours in them. I knew they were all in working order, but I carefully screened the one I thought look the most maintained. It was aircraft number 07. John and I are going into the hangars today to find some equipment.

While I was out this morning, I carefully walked the perimeter fence staying clear of areas where they were lurking on the opposite side. It was a big airfield. On the ground, using my binoculars, I could see movement inside one of the administration buildings on the third floor. Alive? Not sure. I quietly moved back to the tower and alerted John of my find. I was starting to think that the only way to defeat these monsters was to just wait them out. It was like a long prison sentence.

I hadn't thought about my parents for a long time. My hopes weren't too high as to their fate. I thought about taking one of the birds and landing it in a field near my home just so I could get some closure. I could never ask John to come along. It was just a passing thought.

February 4th

~~xxxx~~ 1447 hrs

We fueled one of the T-34s up. Checked the engine, showed John how to work the APU (auxiliary power unit). The T-34c can perform a battery start; it's just best to start it from the external gas powered auxiliary unit. After this, John and I locked Annabelle in the tower and got ready to check out the hangar for any equipment that we may need.

John and I were getting adept at this. He would open the door and I would clear the room. It was a ghost town inside the hangar. John and I edged our way to a room marked, "flight equipment maintenance." The door was halfway open and the lights were on inside. I rushed into the room, weapon ready. I almost shot a dummy that was standing there modeling its flight gear. To small for me, but looked like it would fit John.

After clearing the room, and shutting the door, (just in case) I told John to strip the dummy and try on the flight suit and helmet. I grabbed a helmet off the "maintenance completed" rack and walked over to the test radio to test the boom microphone. It worked fine. We grabbed a couple survival vests, equipped with the bare essentials, as well as one of the wooden model T-34s that might prove useful if I had to explain how something worked to John. There were also sets of keys marked "fuel truck key" hanging on a rack.

After getting back to the tower, I started showing John the basics of flight. I used some flight manuals and the wooden model to give him some idea on avionics and how aircraft control surfaces work. I asked John if he would like to go up and check things out, sort of a recon mission. He agreed and we suited up.

1932 hrs

John and I took off around 1545. We flew northwest at over 200 knots to survey the blast damage. It only took us 40 minutes to get to the outskirts, and that was close enough. The city was rubble. We were at high altitude (over 10,000 ft) to avoid any residual radiation. Decided it best to head back. As soon as we were out of danger we dropped down to an altitude of 2,000 feet. It was a clear day and the sun was at our back. We followed the interstate.

John asked me to roll us over so he could get a good look at the ground. I rolled over about 30-degrees. John and I gazed down to the interstate. These things were making a mass exodus out of the city. I wondered how effective the nukes were on those not in the immediate vicinity. I doubt radiation has any effect on the creatures. Only the heat from the blast could have destroyed them. Minimum safe distance for a living human being would be 150 miles, but not for them. I bet they could survive within twenty miles.

John snapped a digital of the "ghoul's retreat" from the city. We touched down, just as the sun was starting to set, and taxied back to our parking spot near the tower. It truly was a dead place. We saw no sign of life, only thousands and thousands of them walking the landscape. The lights of Corpus Christi would eventually lead them to the city.

February 5th

2201 hrs

They are increasing in number at the west side of the fence. That side is approximately 1/4 of a mile from the tower. Using night vision goggles, I can see them shambling in the distance. The green grainy image is very surreal and disturbing. John and I turned the lights off when we noticed them earlier today. I have a feeling they are the first wave, pushed out of the major cities. Damn, a Geiger counter would have been a good Christmas gift last year. No more frivolous trips in the aircraft. Don't want them getting worked up. I'm going on a scouting mission tonight to the admin building where I saw movement the other day. I have the advantage of night vision, so I think I will be fine. Plus, I need batteries.

February 6th

0430 hrs

I went alone last night to the admin building. John stayed back in the tower. As soon as I left the top floor of the tower, I shut the door and switched to NVGs. The familiar green, grainy image faded in. It made me feel invisible. The building was a good three hundred yards from the tower. I took my rifle for a main weapon, and the Glock for backup. Only took 58 rounds of .223 for the carbine (29 rounds in each magazine). I wasn't heading out to fight a war, just to scavenge. I also took some heavy-duty black zip ties and some rope that I found in the tower. For some reason, I don't think the "me" of a month ago would have left the tower tonight. In the back of my mind, I keep thinking...what is left to live for?

Carefully approaching the front door to the administration building, I began to methodically check the windows for movement. Because of the NVGs limitations, I couldn't see inside the windows until I was close enough to almost hit the building with a thrown rock. I couldn't tell what was moving up on the third floor. I thought for a second that it could be the shadow of an oscillating fan, backlit by a hall light of some sort. That is what I wanted it to be. I was at the front door. It was unlocked. Carefully stepping in, I listened for any possible sound. Reminded me of all the hearing tests I had to take in the military. It was quiet, like a soundproof room inside. After stepping through the second set of doors, I walked into the center of the room and noticed a large staircase that I assume led up to the second and third floors. I took another step and heard a loud crunch beneath my feet. I stepped on a piece of broken glass...an especially loud piece. It was then that I started hearing it.

Sounded like a group of four or five on the floors above me. Low moaning and slow moving feet could be heard moving over the debris above. I knew what it was. They had heard me, and they wanted to come downstairs and dine on my flesh. I quickly spun around and headed back toward the door. Behind me, I heard the sound of one (or more) of them falling down the stairs. Sounded like a garbage bag full of wet leaves.

I sprinted as fast as I could for the door. After making it through the first set of double doors, I quickly pulled out a couple large black zip ties and secured the door. I ran through the next door (outside door) and did the same. They were hard plastic, and I knew they would only slow them down. I put four of them on this door. Just as I was stepping away, they broke through the interior door and started banging on the door I had just secured. I started running back to the tower. I heard the loud, frustrated thuds as I made my escape.

Then the loud crash of a shattered glass. I looked over my shoulder and saw one of them falling out of a third floor window. All the noise must have excited it. I made it to the tower, and ran up the stairs to the top door where John and I were staying. I knocked and yelled through to John to dim the lights and put on his NVGs. After seeing that the crack below the door went dark, I stepped inside to see if the fallen ghoul had chased me.

No sign of it. The door was locked below. I would hear if it tried to gain entrance. We are safe for now.

1534 hrs

John was listening to the radios (he has become depressed over the death of his wife the past few days), and scanning channels when he called me over to check something out. He told me that there was something crawling under one of the planes, but he couldn't see it anymore. I grabbed the binoculars and scanned the area that John was pointing at. It was the corpse that had fallen out of the window last night. It was pulling itself with its arms. Its legs were being dragged motionlessly behind it. I didn't like the idea of going out there and killing it and it wasn't bothering anything right now.

February 7th

1826 hrs

Movement...John and I noticed it a few hours ago. From my angle, I couldn't tell if the admin building door had stayed secure with the zip ties. More of them were gathering on the west end of the fence. Went out to check the plane and make sure it was ready for flight if we needed it to be. I couldn't park the plane too close to the tower after our scouting trip to the city, because of the soft wet grass from a recent rain.

I had to park the plane a good two hundred yards from the tower so it was a trek to go and check on it. I snuck to the plane without incident. I didn't see the crawling ghoul anywhere around. This fenced area was huge and it could be anywhere. The fuel truck was about fifty yards further than the plane. I started walking toward it, and then I saw them. The angle I was standing before blocked my view of them. I counted ten inside the perimeter fence walking around the blind side of the admin building. They didn't see me, but they would see the truck if I tried to pull it to the aircraft to refuel it. My stomach ached at the thought of refueling the aircraft in the dark, but it had to be done.

2100 hrs

I grabbed the NVGs and spare fuel truck keys that John and I found a couple of days earlier, and went out in the dark to refuel the plane. Weapon ready, I slowly glided across the airfield to the fuel truck, this time taking a different angle so that I could see the admin building. No sign of them. Made it to the fuel truck and climbed up to the window and looked inside, (JIC). It was clear. Opened up the door, put it in neutral. I had never tried to push a truck this big, and now I know why. You can't. I was going to have to start the engine. I assume the creatures couldn't see in the dark, but I knew they would hear me.

Reluctantly, I took the key from my pocket and put it in the ignition...I hesitated and then cringing I pushed in the clutch, held the brake and turned the key. After turning it over twice, the engine came to life and I popped the clutch and shot over to the aircraft. On the way, I hit the pump controls inside the vehicle so they would be ready when I jumped out.

Parked the truck, jumped out and started walking toward the plane. I could make out something moving in the grass a hundred yards away. I adjusted the sensitivity on my goggles and saw it. It was the gimpy ghoul in the grass pulling itself toward the tower. I would have to take care of it on my way back.

Then came the blinding flash of John's flashlight through my NVGs from the tower. It was Morse code, to be sure.

B...E...H...I...N...D...

I swung around to see six of them working their way around the fuel truck. I had no choice. I readied my carbine and ran to the aircraft. I jumped up on the wing and started shooting at them. I took out two of them, and missed another.

I was careful not to shoot at the two that were in direct line of sight between the fuel truck and myself. I had two more to take down before I had to carefully handle the other two. Shot another in the head. Its forehead opened up like a spring flower.

The flash from my muzzle was really playing hell in my night vision. I had to adjust the intensifier; it was much darker through the lens as I took down the fourth ghoul with a head and neck shot. There were two more. The two (that were risky to shoot) closed in. They were at the plane. Trying to climb up on the wing. I shot one in the shoulder throwing it off. The other one almost grabbed my boot before I dispatched it with another headshot.

The last wounded ghoul got back on its feet and raised its arms like a deranged Frankenstein as it came at me. I jumped off the wing opposite the monster and watched it as it started walking around the aircraft toward me. It was dark, and the thing just kept running into the wing and empennage of the aircraft. I carefully aimed, as to avoid damage to the bird and let one shot ring out. The jaw tore away from the face, letting the orphaned tongue hang freely. Even in the limited color perception I had with the goggles, it was a disgusting sight. It slumped back and kept coming at me and let out a gurgling sound in its throat. I shot the bastard again, ending its miserable existence.

After dragging all the bodies by the legs, out of the way of the aircraft, I began to refuel it. It took almost ten minutes to top it off.

During this time, I could now hear the moans of the undead carried on the wind. The gunfire excited them. It was a terrible sound. After getting the aircraft refueled, I made for the tower. No detours. Once again the gimp ghoul was nowhere to be seen. WTF? I'm safe inside for the night right now. The moans continue...another night with earplugs.

The thought of the night; I killed six of them...that leaves "gimpy" and another four inside the fence. Where are they?

February 8th
1822 hrs

Awoke this morning to a banging sound on the steel door down stairs. It sounded like more than one of them. John and I crept downstairs to check things out. From the sounds, there were multiple fists banging on the door. Low moans could be heard through the steel. I checked the lock to make sure it was solid. This was the only door in or out of the tower.

The only other way down was a two hundred foot drop from the balcony. John and I brought down a heavy desk to place in front of the door. I went up top and out on the observation deck. I couldn't see down because of the roof over the door area. Using my binoculars, I checked the west fence in the distance. There were more, but the fence was holding. I guessed that the creatures banging on the door were the leftovers from my battle earlier. I don't want to risk opening the door below. I don't know the best way to dispose of them.

February 9th
2142 hrs

The banging stopped last night, and the undead at the bottom of the stairs must have just given up, probably because they never saw us or heard us in here. John and I were still and quiet the whole day yesterday. There was no need to go outside today, as the plane was refueled and we still had power/running water in the tower.

I even got a chance at a shower in the bathroom one floor down. There was a deep sink and a garden hose. The floor panel was plastic and had a drain in the center and the whole room was just a janitor closet, so I rigged the hose up above my head and took a nice shower. Had to use a bar of soap for shampoo, but oh well, beggars can't be choosers, or so they say. I hadn't shaved in a few days. The razor felt good on my face. I felt like a new man after I had washed up. I did some laundry (in the sink with the bar soap) and hung it in the stairwell to dry. I told John about my little hose trick, but he wasn't interested. He just keeps getting worse and worse, grieving over his wife.

I do not know what my long range plans will be. The world is a different place now. The range on the turboprop aircraft is just over four hundred miles. That gives us some options. For a little while today, I actually thought about finding what was left of the military. The questions that they would ask me would be difficult to answer. "How did you survive on the base, son?" I almost feel guilty about not dying with my comrades. It reminds me of a twilight zone episode I saw before the shit hit the fan. It was an episode about a Navy submarine that sank with one survivor. The sailor felt guilty and kept seeing his dead bloated shipmates calling him to the deep.

Please don't let me dream tonight.

February 10th

2350 hrs

The west fence could fail. There are hundreds around the perimeter. The lights of the city have drawn them. I would hate to be shopping in downtown Corpus Christi right now. I have spent most of the day with the binoculars, studying their movements. I saw birds swooping down at some of them. One of the creatures had no arms, and two buzzards were taking advantage of this by perching themselves on the corpse's shoulders and pecking the flesh from its skull. The corpse just gnashed its teeth, snapping at them to no avail. Serves the bastard right.

John and I have tried to figure out what our next step will be, but the safety of the tower has lulled us into a semi-false sense of security. With the limited range on the aircraft, and some areas being radioactive (I'm guessing), it's tough to make a decision. I don't know how to fly a helicopter, so if we found an island, I would need a decent strip of semi-level land to take her down. It has been somewhere in the ballpark of a month since the dead walked. I see signs of decomposition in some of them, but some of them look as though they may have bought the farm recently.

I'm curious as to the effects of ambient radiation on the undead. I know for certain that they would be harmful to the touch, but what effect on the corpse itself? Would the radiation kill the bacteria that caused the corpse to naturally rot? I shudder to think that the bombs dropped could have done more damage than intended good. We are running out of food. We have perhaps a week left. I am sure there is food in some of the surrounding buildings, but I am not prepared at this time to risk my life to get it, as I am certain there are more of those creatures trapped in the confines.

I have been fighting off the shock of this for some time now, and I don't know how much longer it will be before I break down. I suppose it is the natural course of things and I just don't wish to be a basket case at the wrong time. John isn't any better. I played with Annabelle today, as she needed it. She is a good little pup. She can sense that both John and I are on edge, but she doesn't know how to make it better. John and I have decided that one of us needs to be up checking out the perimeter at all times. Going to get some rest and this is not to be confused for sleep. My shift is in four hours.

February 11th
1713 hrs

Using a variation of the square knot, I tied three lengths of one hundred-foot nylon line together to form a sort of escape line, if it were needed. Tying knots into the line every three feet (including the mating knots) caused the three hundred foot length to shorten some, but still allowed it to touch the ground when tied to the balcony and thrown over. I am almost certain these things cannot climb, but still, I pulled the escape rope up and left it neatly coiled outside the balcony door, tied to a sturdy exterior pipe.

The fence is still holding them out, but that is only because they have no evidence that food exists inside. I suppose if they were to see us, or figure out that we were here, they could knock the fence down with ease, making a bad day for John and I. I think we are too far from the west fence for them to see. Cleaned the weapons today, I also showed John how to operate the CAR-15. I also noticed a roof access on the tower. It was probably so that maintenance personnel could get up there and repair the numerous antennas and beacons. I checked it out and climbed up there. It was at least ten feet above the balcony.

I know it has been at least a month since any maintenance has been performed on any of the aircraft, so I went out today, and crept over to the aircraft and pulled out both the pilot and the passenger parachute to make sure they were in good working order. If something happened to the engine, at least John and I would have a choice. I never spotted the loose ghouls that were inside the fence (at least four plus the incapacitated "gimp" creature). Of course, I wasn't looking for them either. I took the parachutes back to the tower. After giving them a good visual inspection, I felt better about taking the plane (number 07) up again, when the need should arise. I keep looking west, making sure our life barrier holds.

February 12th

1913 hrs

There are dead birds on my side of the west fence. I could see them today with my binoculars. I counted six in all. They did not appear eaten; they just look as if they died there. They are on the ground, about four feet from the fence with the mass of the ghouls. I can't tell what kind of bird. They are black, so that rules out most birds of prey. Not a big deal I suppose, but I keep thinking about the black buzzards that were perched on the shoulders of the armless creature, pecking its flesh. Today was uneventful. The fence was still holding.

I am going out tonight to load the extra ammunition/supplies in the avionics bay of the aircraft. I will be especially quiet and leery of the unaccounted for dead that are lurking inside the perimeter. Only one thing drives these creatures, and that is living flesh. I have not seen them attempt to eat each other. Something must be drawing the inner perimeter creatures out of my view. Annabelle is sleeping. I wish I had the carefree thoughts of a dog right now. Ignorance is bliss.

2122 hrs

I'm shaking right now. I haven't been afraid of the dark since I was a child, however my fears were renewed tonight. I loaded the items into the bay of the aircraft. It was cloudy out and barely a moon, so it was pretty dark. It was then that my goggles went black. I had some batteries with me if this happened, but I didn't anticipate the goggles would die that quickly. I fumbled with them in the dark. I was well over a hundred yards from the tower. As I sat there in the dark trying to find where to insert the batteries, I kept hearing shuffling sounds. My mind was playing tricks on me.

The fear was mounting. I finally got the batteries inserted correctly and slammed the NVGs over my head and adjusted the intensifier. As soon as the grainy green image came in, I checked my perimeter. Nothing. This shit is getting to me. I ran back to the tower, up the stairs and sat there. John was looking at one of the charts we had found a few days before. Looking over his shoulder, I saw a place that he had circled. "Mustang Beach" was not very far from us at all.

February 13th

2013 hrs

It's dark outside, and very cold, especially up here in the tower. I suppose if we were to turn on the lights it would warm things up, but it would also excite the creatures on the other side of the west fence. I'm sure they would see it. I went up to the roof access at sundown, and marveled at the stars. There weren't any lights on inside of the perimeter, (John and I had taken care of this when the dead started massing on the west fence) and this made for a fine view of the Milky Way.

I think John is pulling out of his emotional low, and starting to recover. He actually joked around with me today. I didn't leave the confines of the tower today, but I do need to get those parachutes back to the aircraft so we have less to carry when we leave. I'm still sort of freaked out about last night, so I guess it can wait until later. It is still puzzling to me why the creatures are on the west end of the fence, and no other. I would love to have some real food. When monitoring the radios today, John heard a broadcast from an Air Force aircraft scouting the area. One key thing that John noted that disturbed me, the pilot had to turn back to base because he wanted to conserve his fuel. The pilot remarked about the limited supply back on the base. This tells me they are rationing jet fuel; therefore, they are confined to an area where it is not readily available. The government (or this part of it) is trapped just like we are.

An island off the coast of Texas is starting to sound better and better. The only problem is that supplies would be difficult to come by with just the two of us scavenging.

February 14th
1440 hrs

The fence is buckling inward and I don't know how much longer it will hold. It's today or nothing. Looking at the windsock, there is a strong wind blowing east to west toward the airstrip. We will take to the air as soon as

Tower

February 15th
2243 hrs

Situation is dire. My bleeding has stopped, but I'm still light headed from all the blood loss. It must have been right before I was writing my last entry yesterday when they broke through. I did not notice they were inside the perimeter until 1445, by then it was too late. John and I saw them. The fence was down in about a hundred-meter section and they were pouring into the airfield like runner ants.

We gathered the necessities (what we thought were needed anyway) and started out the door to get in the bird and leave. As we reached the bottom and opened the door, there were four of them there waiting on John and I. We slammed the door shut and pushed the desk in place in front of the entry that we had brought down days before.

We were fucking trapped like rats and those bastards could sense it. It wasn't long before the moans of hundreds could be heard below and the constant banging on the only exit door started. This tower was over two hundred feet high and only one way out. I went outside on the balcony, and my suspicions were confirmed.

There were literally three hundred of them congregated around the exterior door as well as the covered area of the tower. John muzzled Annabelle, because she was starting to go nuts. I grabbed the rope and looked below to see where it would hit when I threw it. No joy. Sadly, I pulled the rope back up on the balcony, as there was no way we were making it down that rope without a hundred of them seeing us and taking us out before we even touched the ground.

It was then that the situation worsened. The sound of bending, aching steel could be heard below. There were so many of them, the masses were pushing their way through. At that moment, I knew we were fucked. I looked at John and told him, "I'm not ready to die yet." He said, "Me neither." and we both rushed over to the door that led down the stairs and started throwing TVs, desks and chairs down the stairs. That would buy us a little time. We then shut the door... —It opened outward, thank god.

The upstairs door was not as sturdy as the bottom exterior door. Just as we got the door shut and the last remaining desk in front of it, we could hear the metal clanging of dress shoes on the stairs. John shoved Annabelle in his backpack and zipped her up to her neck. I motioned for John to get to the top of the ladder and wait for me to start passing up supplies.

John waited with Annabelle in his pack at the top rung. She could sense our fear and was whimpering. First, I passed him the two most important items of my plan... —The two parachutes that I never put back in the aircraft! Then I passed up a six-pack of water bottles, then the NVGs, then a few packs of MREs. Just for some odd novelty, I passed up my case with my small laptop. Lastly, all our weapons and much of our ammunition, although shooting every last round would still leave hundreds here to deal with.

They were at the upstairs door now. This door had a rectangular shaped vertical window, about six by ten inches. I could see one of them with its face pressed up to the shatterproof glass, sneering, trying to see what was inside. It started pounding and moaning when it saw me. The others soon followed suit. John climbed up onto the roof and I followed. It was windy like the day before. This was good news, maybe.

John took his pack (and his dog) off his shoulders and turned it around so it was being worn in the front of his body. I helped him put the parachute on and, using zip-ties, I strapped as much to him as I could without hindering too much movement. I quickly showed him the basics on how to get out of the parachute when he hit the ground.

I explained to him that it was very important that he unfasten the two inner thigh straps prior to the chest strap. He nodded that he got it, so I bent down and grabbed my chute. The broken glass sound erupted from below and I was sure they pushed the shatterproof glass through the doorframe. I hoped that these things could not climb ladders. Using the carabiners from my daypack, I secured the rifle to my chest d-ring through the carrying handle. My knife was strapped to my belt for easy access when I hit the ground.

I would be jumping first...at this moment came the familiar sound of bending steel, and the screeching sound of the wood desk being launched across the floor. There was no way to secure the top hatch from the outside. It was simple, if they could climb, they would get up here. I gave one last lesson to John... "Make sure you pull your risers to slow your descent." I described what they looked like to him.

I made John watch me as I crept to the edge of the roof. I could hear the sounds of them wondering below, trying to find their food. I could see the balcony door below me being pushed open, two, five, and now twelve creatures were wondering the balcony below. For some reason, they didn't look as rotted as I thought they should be. I was guessing that every bit of two-hundred walking dead were inside the tower at that moment.

John leaned over and saw them. He was white with fear. Not just the thought of being eaten to death...but the thought of jumping the tower, breaking both legs, and not being able to give yourself a fighting chance...I knew what he was thinking. I was thinking the same thing. At that moment the hatch on the roof access jumped up and slammed back down... Clang...clang...The creature's wedding ring was chiming on the hatch, making it rise a couple inches then slam back down, as the back of its left hand hit. I could see the white hand for a split second when the weight of the hatch pushed it back down. I almost fucking lost it.

I somehow grabbed John's attention through this and showed him how to pull the release d-ring for the drogue. The drogue is a small parachute that catches the wind and pulls the rest of the chute out. The drogue on this chute is spring powered. Pull the pin, and the drogue will shoot out, catching the wind, and deploy the rest of the chute. I checked the windsock on the far side of the field...good to go. Looked below. There were many, but most of them seemed to be in the tower. I pulled the pin and held on to the ledge, so I wouldn't fall off before it deployed.

The wind caught the main chute and literally yanked me off my feet. I could see the roof hatch swing completely open and heard it bash as it jack-knifed and hit the roof. John was right behind me. The creatures on the balcony saw John and I jump, and started almost screaming. I looked up as their outstretched hands reached for the dome of my chute.

There were windows every few feet that looked in/out of the stairwell. Damn...they were climbing over each other to get to the top. Many were in military uniforms. My estimate at two hundred was too low. From the way they were piled on top of each other in the stairwell, there were more than likely a thousand of them. I was slowly floating to the ground, it seemed like forever. Every window that I passed by on the way down was another snapshot, or Picasso if you will of dead faces and limbs crowded together...Then it was back to reality as I hit the ground. It wasn't a soft landing, but I didn't break anything. I immediately unlatched my chute and rolled out of it. I unsheathed my knife and waited for John to hit the ground. The creatures were closing in.

As soon as John hit, he was attempting to get out of the chute. Neither of us wanted the wind dragging us into a group of those things. I had to help him along by slicing through the nylon harness. I told John to grab one end of the chute. We then ran through a group of those things toward the aircraft.

John knew what my plan was. We wrapped at least ten of those things up in the damaged chute by running around them and tangling up the cut harness with the drogue. Luckily, we drifted fifty meters in the direction of the aircraft when we jumped. We ran as fast as we could. In all the excitement, the dog slipped out of John's pack onto the ground. John was ahead of me, and I scooped her up on my way. She was so scared that she was trying to climb on top of my head. I don't fucking blame her. I felt the warmth of urine seeping through my clothing. She pissed herself. *

We made it to the aircraft and I slung open the cockpit glass and threw my shit in the back seat. John and Annabelle jumped in the back and I told John to strap in. I immediately jumped in the bird and slid the cockpit closed and latched the lock. I remembered the startup sequence from the checklist, and out of habit started saying it aloud as I performed it...

Come to think of it, it might have been me.

"1_Clock started
2_Starter switch on
3_Battery above ten volts
4_Ignition light on
5_Fuel pressure light out
6_Oil pressure rising
7_N1 above 12 percent
8_Condition lever to feather
9_Thumbs up to the lineman."

I almost laughed at myself on this step. There was no lineman. Although I was sure the bastard was out there somewhere looking for us. I increased the condition lever to full bite and could feel the propeller catch air.

I couldn't have avoided what happened next. There were fifty of them closing in on us. All I could do was to attempt to get into take off position. One of them near the nose walked toward the prop. I always wondered what it would sound like, now I knew; like a big vegetable processor. That corpse lost its whole left shoulder in the deal. I checked my prop RPM, it dipped a little but cycled back up to 2200 RPM. I didn't want to hit any more of them. Using the pedals, I weaved the nose in and out of corpses as I rolled into position, buzzing a few of them, but nothing big like the first one.

I checked my fuel pressure, good to go, everything was in the green. I pushed my power lever to max and I started my take off roll...50 knots, the airspeed indicator kicked in...65 knots, 70 knots... I clipped one of them with my left wing, breaking its hip (at least) right before 80 knots. At 85 knots I pulled the stick back and we were airborne. John already had his helmet fastened; I grabbed mine from my lap and pulled it over my head. I checked the internal communications system with John. He was reading me but I could tell that he was in some sort of shock by the way he was talking and by the fact that his lips looked blue in the rear view mirror.

The worst part of this was that we had no real place to go. As we took off, I looked over at the tower. The roof was now full of them and they were walking off of the top of it like lemmings. I was trying to fly the plane and look at the chart at the same time. I was wobbling back and forth, and could hear John getting airsick on the speakers in my helmet. It was sort of funny, but I didn't want to laugh at him. I noticed a small abandoned airstrip called "Matagorda Island airfield" about 65 miles northeast of our position. I quickly marked it on my chart with a red ink pen. It looked like there were numerous islands there, and it wasn't too far from Corpus, so the power was probably still on.

We cruised northeast for about twenty-minutes at 180 knots when I started having propeller trouble. The engine was fine, but the prop kept losing pitch angle thus not allowing it to grab as much air. In short, it kept feathering on me. I knew this was something to do with the corpse I chopped up earlier. I had no choice. I had to glide the plane in, because the prop pitch control was probably losing oil pressure. I feathered the prop with the condition lever and pulled the engine back to three hundred foot pounds of torque.

According to my chart, the strip was in sight but I couldn't see it. I descended to three thousand feet to get a good glide solution. Below me it looked like a tourist area, with numerous hotels lining the beach. Thank god it was February and not tourist season. At this point, I had to make a choice. I could either find another place to land, or say fuck it, and land in the street. Below, I could see a few of the creatures, but it was nothing like what we were running from. I was on borrowed time without a good propeller. I had to take her down. I pulled the stick back and left and pushed a little left rudder and glided into a 180-degree rendezvous with the road below. Nose down, gear down, and as soon as I was near the road, I flared my nose up and touched down with my main landing gear.

I hit the brakes and tried to steer my wings between the telephone poles. I still had a lot of fuel left and didn't want to be wearing flaming fuel because my wing decided to wrap itself around a poll. Along the way, I clipped one of those creatures with my right wing, doubling it over. It had hit its head so hard when it slammed its upper body into the wing that it died instantly, leaving a brown smudge of brain on the wing. I checked my speed, fifty knots...As I slowed to a halt, the immediate area was clear.

I signaled John to get out. I left the engine running so that the sound of the aircraft would muffle our escape. John and I jumped out, grabbed our shit and headed for a sign called "Matagorda Island Marina."

Now here we are...

I gashed my leg open on the sharp bumper of a wrecked car five minutes into the journey. It was a long hump, (a mile's worth of side streets, beach fronts, and backyards) but we are here. It is a decent sized marina with a large ferry, and a gift shop. Electricity is still on. Marina abandoned. Looks like the harbormaster took his own life. His bloated corpse is slumped over a desk in the front office, with what was left of his brain caked on a calendar marked January. The TV was still on, playing snow.

February 16th
1912 hrs

I am very weak today. If it were not for John, I would be dead. Annabelle is next to me sleeping. It is dark outside and I have been blacking out on and off most of the day. My leg is infected and I need some antibiotics. In the harbormaster's desk, we found some whiskey. This has served me most of the day as a disinfectant, as well as painkiller. Tomorrow, John will go out alone to find some medicine for my infection. We are in no trouble currently.

I could hear the sound of the aircraft engine still running yesterday for at least two hours before it died. No matter, it was junk now anyway, as I am sure there is no one left alive that knows how to fix it.

February 17th

2220 hrs

I'm feeling better today. We heard the sound of an engine in the distance that sounded like it could have been a dirt bike. John found a first-aid kit on the ferry near here. It didn't have any pill antibiotics, but it did have some of the topical kind. I have been keeping the wound clean and washing it a few times a day, and applying the medicine. It seems to be working. I'm just still very red and sore around the cut. Last night we heard the sounds of something in the darkness. Using the goggles, we tried to spot it, but it turned out it was only a raccoon looking for food. Tomorrow, I will try and walk so I don't get too stiff. John and I need to survey this area, as we are only safe here temporarily.

"Dark Knight"

February 18th

2302 hrs

There are sporadic gunshots in the wind. We picked up a distress call on the harbor radio from a family in the outskirts of Victoria, TX (50 miles from current location). The signal was faint and we tried to respond, however they could not hear us as they kept transmitting over and over as if we weren't there. I thought about it and decided that it would not be worth a fifty-mile trek through hostile territory to find a group of people that may be dead when I got there. Sad. I used to be more compassionate and chivalrous. I guess after seeing bad things happen to good people, you just don't want to be good. They are trapped in an attic with those things shuffling around below. I think I know who will be able to wait longer.

I guess they must have moved the essentials up to the attic when the "S.H.T.F." Something keeps eating at me, as if a shell of my former self were ordering me to do something. Or, maybe I do have a conscience left. Doubt it.

I am walking now, but not running. John and I unfastened the chain that held the floating ramp to the marina. We found some rope in the utility room of the marina office, and use it as part of our drawbridge mechanism. John and I thought of it today. When we are here, we simply pull the rope, and the floating ramp gets pulled away from the shore to the marina, making a hard time for any of those fuckers to get here. I hope they can't swim.

February 19th

1524 hrs

We are making good headway in securing the area. There are numerous small boats in the marina, and John and I have pulled the ones we think are worth a damn to our location. I want to check them all at once to avoid starting the engines at different times, making too much noise. This morning I saw a group of eight dead pass the street about fifty meters from the water's edge. The only thing that troubled me was that they were moving faster than the previous creatures we have encountered. By no means were they running or even jogging, but they definitely were not walking. My heart sank as I noticed the speed at which they moved.

I crossed the gangway to the ferry next to the marina office. It was a medium sized ferry that could fit about twenty vehicles. I assume it was used to cross the channel to mainland Texas.

I climbed to the top deck and checked the bridge. I found a set of binoculars (left my others at the tower) and used them to try and spot the pack of dead. I looked up and down the beach, and checked the windows on the hotels. No signs of life. I counted five windows on the fifth and sixth floor in the nearest hotel (Hotel La Blanc) that did have occupants. Dead, rotting occupants that will never check out of their hotel.

These binoculars were built for sea service. They are large, heavy and had powerful magnification. They're not really suitable to carry around, but great for checking the area. Three of the monsters just stood there at the window staring out. One of them seemed as if it looked right at me. The two others looked like they were pacing the room. I wonder how they died.

My leg is much better now and I think I will be able to run on it if need be in a couple days. We are out of food today, so we are going to burgle the vending machines until I can run again. Then we will scavenge for food. I could only salvage 500 rounds for the CAR-15. John has a thousand for the semi-auto .22.

2223 hrs

Thirty minutes ago I heard a noise. I donned the night vision goggles on and expected to see another raccoon. Not the case this time. Four of them are standing at the waters edge looking out toward our location. They aren't making any noise. They are just standing there with arms swinging ominously at the waters edge. John and I are being as quiet as possible. I am conserving battery power by leaving the goggles off, but it seems every splash the water makes as it hits the marina pontoons, I imagine them swimming toward us.

February 20th

1854 hrs

I was up all night last night. The fog on the water made it impossible for me to see the shore after midnight. This morning when the sun came up and burned some of the fog away, I checked for them. I could hear some noise in the distance. It sounded like someone was knocking over tin cans. My leg is feeling much better. Today, we lived off of stale candy bars and soft drinks. Makes me think...There will probably never be another can of this made. Sort of depressing. I'm going to need a watch soon, as the battery in this one has been the same for over two years. I guess I will put that on the list of "must loot." Although, some would argue that stealing to stay alive is not looting. I say its just details. I'm not planning to raid a jewelry store but I wont turn down something that will keep me alive.

On a lighter note, John and I found a radio station still broadcasting music. Too bad it's automated and it keeps looping every twelve hours. Still good for morale and I'm glad it's still working. You can almost imagine it is live. It helps...a little.

February 21st
0800 hrs

We are in dire need of provisions. Plenty of water here at the marina in the drinking water dispenser, but we have been living off of caffeine and sugar. A detailed map of this area would be very helpful, although getting to it may prove fatal. Early this morning as the sun was rising through the fog, I could hear and see many of them walking the street in front of the ferry marina. For some reason they were moving together. Seemed like they were attracting themselves to the noise they were making. I couldn't see the whole group of them, but from the numbers I did see, I could estimate that there were hundreds.

John and I picked the best boat out of the few that we rounded up a few days ago. I checked the fuel tank and saw that it was 3/4 full. There was a fuel pump on the marina, so decided to see if it still worked. Went into the marina office, and checked for a pump switch. Number two pump switch was still on.

I went out to use pump number two to fill the boat up. No joy, the pump worked; however no fuel came forth. It must have been drained when the shit went down. I went back inside to flip pump number one back on line. Squeezed the nozzle and it pumped for a few seconds before any fuel came out. A nice rainbow of fuel was present on the surface of the water. In another time, that might have cost me a fine. A few seconds of pumping and the last 1/4 of fuel was added. I found a couple empty plastic gas cans in the marina, filled those and tied them into the boat.

John went back in and grabbed my rife and held it at the ready toward the shore while I worked. We still had no idea what capabilities the dead had when it came to water. Yesterday, while listening to the last radio music broadcasts of mankind, John and I found a metal key box next to a shelf in the administration office. All of the watercraft had a registration number stuck to the side of their hulls with reflective number tape, so finding the key was not a difficult task. I matched the number with the key marked 'Shamrock 220' and went back out to her to give it a shot.

The back end had drifted, facing the admin office door when I walked out. The boat's name was painted on the rear with a half-circle type banner. It was the "Bahama Mama." I jumped on to the stern and walked over to the wheel and inserted the key. John was still sitting on the dock, eyes trained toward the strips of hotels and the street. I slid the throttle to the start position, and turned the key. On the second attempt it started with no problems and I let it run for about five minutes.

I sat there smiling at John at how lucky we had been. I turned the key to the 'off' position and just as the engine died down, we heard what it had been drowning out. A football stadium of hideous moans echoed throughout the buildings on the island. We could hear Annabelle's reaction from inside the marina. She was upset at the noise, and the hair on the back of my neck was standing up. Now that the engine worked without any doube, it was time to plan a trip to gather supplies. Leaving in the morning.

February 22nd

0403 hrs

As the day went by yesterday, the shoreline was home to over fifty of those things, begging for our flesh. Something just isn't right about them. Their numbers have dwindled to roughly twenty. Bahama Mama and co. leaving for supplies.

Exodus of the Bahama Mama

February 23rd
2006 hrs

Using the night vision goggles, I prepped the boat for an early departure yesterday morning. It was around 0430 when I started loading candy bars, bottled water, ammunition, and extra fuel cans onto the boat. I brought a pry bar also, in case we had to strong arm our way into a place. John was prepping our little man made sanctuary for Annabelle. It would be dangerous to take her with us. She would be fine here in the confines of our little floating hide away.

The twenty or so dead were still walking the shoreline, blind to the night, and hoping for a glimpse of prey. I found some plastic oars inside the maintenance shed and quietly put them in the boat (never know). John and I boarded the craft and I untied us. I reluctantly started the engine and checked the movement on the shoreline. Some of the creatures were flailing wildly and two of them were wading the water up to their knees. The fact that their fear of water was dwindling sent chills up my spine.

As we pulled out, I navigated west. I found a chart used for water navigation in the office at the marina. Too bad there wasn't a map of Matagorda Island in there also. I knew the general shape of the island, however, I had no idea of the details. I was now heading toward San Antonio bay. I was going slow, conserving fuel and watching out for any dangers that may appear in the light morning fog.

My choices were clear according to the sea chart. I would sail into San Antonio bay and choose either the west, or the east shore. To the west was the small (according to chart) coastal town of Austwell, and east was Seadrift. Neither John nor I were familiar with either. We both agreed on Seadrift. No particular reason. Perhaps in the back of my mind, I thought that because of its name, it would be a better suited docking point.

The sun was peaking up over the east horizon and was at our backs when Seadrift came into sight. There were numerous long docks, no doubt to provide berth for fishing vessels. I cut the engine and John and I started rowing toward the docks. Noise was a luxury we could not afford.

Using the binoculars taken from the large ferry, I scanned the coastline. They were here. I could see their pitiful frames walking aimlessly up and down the main street that ran the length of the bay. There weren't many, but enough to be trouble. The sign for the marina read, "Dockside Fishing Center." One of the boats berthed here held a deadly crew. John and I saw three of the creatures walking the deck of the fishing boat, only forty meters away. They saw us, and one of them lunged out at us falling off the boat, disappearing into the murky waters of the bay.

As we rowed closer to the dock, it appeared that there was a small grocery and bait store right off the pier. At arms length of the tie down, I secured the Mama to the dock. John and I carefully stepped onto the worn wooden planks of the pier. I grabbed the pry bar and stuck it under my belt. Every creak seemed like thunder. The sound of the dead walking on the other boat was much louder than we were, but it was still quiet. There were no sounds of nature and no engines; even the bay water splashing on the shore seemed muted.

The gangway to the boat containing the two remaining ghouls was still in place. They were a threat. I had John keep their attention. He waved his arms at them as I snuck over to the gangway (plank) linking the boat to the dock and quietly slid it into the water. The splash was louder than I expected, and they immediately turned toward me and let out the all too familiar moan. Crabs lined the deck of the fishing vessel with the two corpses. Dead fish could be seen in a pile on the stern.

The stink was incorrigible. The crabs were snapping at the pant legs of the dead. There were several crab carcasses littering the deck. Legs were pulled off and shells were cracked. Upon a closer look at the undead creatures, I could see that several of their teeth were missing or broken. The bastards were trying to eat the crabs.

John and I left the motley crew of ghouls and headed for the grocery store. Weapons ready, we approached the front door. No movement. Damn I was hungry. Just thinking about all of the food in there made it worse. In my right arm I had my rifle at the ready, in my left I tightly held the black steel pry bar. The little grocery store was no bigger than a tennis court. Hurricane shudders were in place prohibiting any view of the inside except through the glass front door. Two signs hung on the inside of the door. "Closed," and "Help Wanted." The latter was an understatement.

Walking up to the door, I grabbed the handle and pulled. No dice. It was going to have to be the hard way. Using the bar, I slid it between the door and the frame and began prying. I wasn't going to be surprised this time. I thought back to that Wal-Mart. Seemed like ages ago. I nervously watched the inside for movement, as I grunted and struggled with the locked door. John was becoming a good point man. He was scanning for movement, covering me. Finally after a few minutes of struggling with the door, I finally got it open.

The store was dark and it was very warm inside. I could smell rotten fruit. I turned the light on that was mounted on my weapon. I panned the area, listening for anything out of the ordinary. John and I each grabbed carts and made our way to the canned goods section. Quietly we filled our carts with anything that could be eaten, and drank, starting with non-perishables first. All the bread was moldy, but some of the cookies were still good. Of course, the canned goods were fine.

The refrigerator section was totally rotten. I panned my light through the glass and saw the yellow looking gallon milk jugs, and molded cheese. Then something else caught my eye. There was movement in the freezer. I always knew there was walk space back there for the stock-boys to stock the cold goods. It appears that the stock-boy and another friend were still in there. The light excited them and I could see them pounding on the shelves full of milk. In one section, one of them was crawling through the shelf to the refrigerator door that led to us.

John and I decided that it was time to leave. We wheeled our carts back to the front and I checked the area for any signs the enemy. I opened the front door and John wheeled out first. As I followed, I could see the refrigerator door open at the back of the store, and heard the sound of a body falling to the floor. I knew it was Mr. Stock-boy wanting to check and see if we were finding everything all right.

John and I hurriedly jogged back down toward the pier. The carts were making a lot of noise, and I didn't wish to wait around and see how things worked out. Quickly, we loaded the boat with the provisions. Behind us the front door to the grocery store was creeping open and I could see the pale figure of the creature that was in the refrigerator section. John and I jumped in the boat, and I kicked us away from the dock. We paddled as fast as we could, and stopped about ten meters out from where we were tied up.

It was time for a break. Using my knife, I opened up a can of cold beef stew and drank down the contents. John did the same. As we sat there drinking bottled water, our friend on the pier was giving us a warm bon voyage. The creature looked horrible, it was missing a right hand, and most of the jaw. It was wearing a long white apron with something written on it in blood. I pulled out my binoculars and in simple block letters it read:

"If you can read this, kill me!"

I smiled at this and thought to myself that I would have liked to have known this man when he was alive, as I appreciated his sense of humor. I slung my weapon to my shoulder and selected single shot. I then took aim, and shot stock-boy in the head. John gave me a "why did you do that?" look, and I just glanced at him and said, "Professional courtesy my friend, professional courtesy."

The trip back to our marina stronghold was uneventful. About a quarter mile from the pier, we cut the engines and quietly rowed to the dock. There weren't any of them on the shore, probably because they followed the sound of our engines away from the marina early this morning. We quietly unloaded most of the food and water. It was dinnertime for Annabelle. It's funny how she probably eats better now than she did before all of this.

February 24th
2047 hrs

John and I talked about family. I told him that I was worried about mine, and that I doubted they lived through this, even considering their location. John told me about his son and about how proud he was of him, and how he had gotten a scholarship to Purdue. He went on to tell me the antics of his recent family reunion and how his wife couldn't get along with his mother. John asked me why I joined the service. I told him my story of how I was a poor country boy from small town, USA that wanted to serve his country, and how I came up the hard way through the enlisted ranks.

(Not that it matters now what my rank is anyway.)

I'm sure somewhere deep underground in the northwest United States, rank still matters, but not here on this two-bit marina on some no name island. I went on to tell John why I didn't stay with my comrades at the base. I paused at this, questioning to myself whether or not I should have fought the good fight. I told John that sometimes I regret not going to the base with my fellow officers. The point of the matter is, I'm alive and they are not. I would rather choose <u>needle in a haystack over jackass in a fortress.</u> I expressed to him that I would have to live with my decision, but at least I'm alive to do it.

John looked at me and said, "You speak as if I am accusing you of desertion." I apologized and told him that it was a sensitive subject. I guess I am a deserter. Who is alive to tell? I suppose if things ever get back to normal, I will...No use thinking about that.

My heartstrings tugged at the thought of my parents being board up in their attic, praying for help. My imagination could almost see their dirty clothes, matted hair and malnutrition-riddled frames. I had to compartmentalize this thought to keep from making a bad decision. Willingly attempting to save my parents whom are hundreds of miles away would be suicide. I wonder how long it took for the devastation to reach the back woods of Arkansas? It didn't take long from the time I saw it on the news to the time it was outside on my street, clawing at my wall.

It is a cold decision to make; however if I wish to live, I cannot let emotion tell me where to point my steps. Even in the best case, a minor lapse in judgment would mean death. If I chose to go to Arkansas to see if my parents still lived, every decision would have to be perfect, right down to where I chose to sleep at night, and where I chose to scavenge for supplies.

What went wrong? I don't know why it has taken me almost two months to really think about it, but what sick fuck would do something like this? I assume too much. Was man reaching the level of deity? Maybe it was something larger. I don't want to think about that right now, as I would only curse and scream, and if it was something bigger, I didn't want to take the chance of this higher force reprimanding me for being insubordinate. So for now, I guess we will have our little unspoken agreement. If you exist, lets just leave each other alone...I'll let you know when I'm ready.

I don't fear the reaper.

February 25th
1932 hrs

The coast was clear earlier today when I took Annabelle out to stretch her legs on the dock. I walked her up and down the wooden planks. I could tell she had put on a couple pounds and needed a little exercise. I kept her muzzle on to avoid any loud barking. The marina resembled a system of docks that would look like an "H" from the air. The floating marina office was attached to one side of the "H" and a single, floating ramp was the only thing that formerly connected this artificial island of wood, metal and foam to the real island.

I walked her around the perimeter of the dock. Yesterday, I took a long fishing pole from one of the boats and tried to touch the bottom from the point on the dock closest to the shore. I couldn't touch, so that meant that the water was at least nine feet deep in that area. For some reason I feared that they might be able to wade the water and just climb up here. I felt a little more assured after my depth finder test.

On our second walking lap around the marina, Annabelle started sniffing the wind, and the familiar scene of her hair standing up on her back became obvious. She sensed them. The wind was blowing from the shore, and we were downwind. I picked her up and took her inside. I went to the window facing the shoreline and waited. I told John what she had done while we were outside. John and I shared the window, and just kept watching.

The sounds came first and it reminded me of the sound of a distant street sweeper being carried by the wind. Then the mass of them came slowly stumbling and even walking by. There was no way to count them, and I knew that if they wanted, they could get to us here on the marina. When I saw them pass by our location, it reminded me of a big city marathon. All it would take would be the sheer number of them piling themselves up on the water. I was getting tired of running, but this is a big island, and I'm sure that we could never find enough weapons or ammunition to kill them all. If only we had a few more days back at the tower in Corpus to plan. John is picking up faint signals from the survivors trapped in the attic. That is another thing that is getting at me.

February 26th

0923 hrs

John and I were monitoring the radios this morning. It seems our attic survivors are still ok. We are still unable to raise them with our transmitter. The man's name is William Grisham, and he is making all of the broadcasts. From time to time, I have heard a female voice in the background, but I can't tell if it is a child or his wife. He says that they are not infected and have enough food and water to last a week, but the sounds of the corpses below are driving them mad.

He doesn't seem to think that they can make it out alive without help. Looking at the air chart that I still have, we could take the boat back to Seadrift, then find a car there and try to make it the rest of the way to Victoria, TX. I don't even know why I'm thinking this. The whole trip looks like about fifty miles. Ten of which are on the water. That means eighty miles of round trip danger. I can't ask John to go and actually, I would prefer that he stayed here. John is torn between doing the right thing and possibly losing his fellow survivor, or doing the wrong thing and losing his soul. My thoughts are happening in phases. I would hate to be in that position, but I was in that position and I did something about it. I chose to live.

2145 hrs

William has been broadcasting off and on all day. He sounds desperate. I can't stop listening because it is another human voice. His maddening ramblings are bringing my mind into a maze of darkness. I feel I must help. John and I have discussed it at length, and he will stay and hold down the fort with Annabelle. I almost feel like I am starting to get to know William. For some odd reason, he rambled on for about thirty minutes just talking about whatever was on his mind. I assume that shock may be setting in and he is using the radio as an emotional outlet. He spoke of his job, and how he was a chemist before all of this happened. I listened to his voice, and could almost hear his honesty and integrity about the fear of losing his family. I feel I MUST help. Tonight I will prepare and tomorrow I will go.

February 27th

0820 hrs

Leaving shortly. I will be taking the boat back to Seadrift, then the rest either by car, or on foot. This could take a few days. I found a CB radio on one of the boats here. It's a little heavy, and battery powered, but when I get within range of William's radio, I will use it to try and hail him. No use going the last twenty miles only to find William and family as one of them. I have nearly 500 rounds left from what I salvaged in my rush from the control tower, taking into account the one round used to shoot the stock boy in the head. With the radio, water, weapon, rounds, food, and other small miscellaneous gear, I am carrying over 70 lbs. This is why a car would be preferable.

My plan is to acquire a road atlas when I get to Seadrift, then "shadow" the roads all the way to Victoria (If I am on foot). I can't risk being seen by anything living or dead along the way. I will stay in contact with John as long as the hand held will transmit. I do not know its transmit range, but I am sure I could talk to him from Seadrift, as the signal will travel further over the water.

Last night I was outside looking at the stars when I saw bright green streak in the sky, similar to a shooting star. The green was probably the copper burning up inside a satellite that has long been forgotten. Only a matter of time before GPS fails, along with all other satellite based services.

Enough useless babble.

Time to cock the hammer.

1844 hrs

I paddled the boat out to about 1/4 of a mile distance from the marina, as to not attract them to John. Had to gas up the boat last night. When I turned on the engine, I cruised west a bit to attract them away from the marina, just to give John a little more peace of mind. Didn't take long for me to reach Seadrift, as it is only about ten miles from the marina to the mainland Texas. Once again, I shut the Bahama Mama down and did my best to paddle (with one oar) the rest of the way. When I reached the same marina John and I were at a few days before, I noticed that the same two creatures on the fishing boat, and the re-dead stock boy face down on the dock. He was being picked apart by a group of birds.

Before approaching any of the docks, I tried the CB radio on the pre-selected channel that John and I agreed on. After the second attempt, I heard John's faint crackling voice asking me if everything was ok. I told him that everything was fine, and that his friends on the fishing boat were having crab this evening, and wondered if he would be attending. He laughed at this and I told him that I would get back to him as soon as I got back into range.

I knew that there was another creature inside the grocery store. I could see faint movement on the street about 1/4 of a mile north inland. I could see what looked like another set of marina docks further up the shoreline. It was too far to paddle without another oarsman. I had to start the engine. This excited the creatures on the fishing boat and it felt as if every set of eyes left in the world were staring at me... —Angry for the broken silence.

As I sped up the coastline, the creatures on the beach took notice of my boat and started following me up the waterline. I couldn't believe what I was seeing. These creatures were not the same, slow shambling creatures I was used to. Some of them seemed to move faster.

One of them appeared to be almost trotting, with its arms reaching out toward my boat. They were still very uncoordinated, and many of them were falling face down in the sand, only to get back up to pursue me. I decided to distance myself from the shoreline and approach the dock in a manner that would not attract this rag tag bunch to my position.

I took the boat a mile out into the center of the bay and approached the dock in a perpendicular direction. I tried to build up enough speed so that when I cut my engine, I could drift at least most of the way. Not being familiar with this dock, my weapon was at the ready as I inched closer. It was very similar to the east dock in many ways. I saw no dead in this area. There was a gas station in plain view about 300 meters from the marina. I shuddered when I thought of being on the roof of the last gas station back home. My fear started to grow as the view to the gas station became clear.

I finally cut the engine and drifted as far as I could without using the paddle. I eased in to the marina, and tied the boat down. I checked the area for immediate danger, and then checked the fuel level to make sure I had enough to make it back to Matagorda island. I turned the CB radio off, as I didn't want any calls breaking the precious silence I was trying to maintain. Shouldering my heavy pack I stepped up on the dock and began to walk toward the shore, taking extra precaution to watch my footing, and minimize noise.

I could see two vehicles parked in front of the gas station. One of the cars still had the fuel nozzle attached to it, as if the owner never got the chance to place it back on the pump. I could see that the other car, parked in front of the gas station, had the driver's side door open. I knew for sure that the dome light would have drained the battery long before I got here.

I made my way closer to the station, weapon ready. I knew that if I had to evade, I wouldn't be able to go for more than three miles without rest, as it was a chore to move with all the weight. As I approached the car near the pumps, the only sounds I could hear were the sounds of the water churning near the docks. I was at the pump.

I checked the gallons readout on the pump to see if the car had actually been filled up. No joy, it was digital and the power to the pumps was shut off. Quietly, I took the nozzle out of the car and placed it on the ground, then put the fuel cap back on. My best guess was that the car was a mid 80's model. The decals told me the car was a Buick Regal Grand National. It was black.

I went around to the driver's side door. The window was open, so I reached inside to check for keys. No keys. I made for the convenience store. The glass display windows and door were shattered, looted long ago. I wasn't there to loot; —I just needed a road atlas. I could see the map display on the same counter as the microwave, so I ducked through the broken glass and headed that way. My nose didn't warn me of any dead here. I scanned each aisle as I made for the maps. They were fresh out of road atlases, but I did find a laminated road map of Texas. Since I didn't plan on taking any interstate trips, this would do just fine.

It was now time to deal with the keyless Buick. Since this area seemed devoid of current danger, I decided it best to attempt to hot wire the car, rather than attempt to find a working car in dangerous territory. I knew that I would be S.O.L. on a newer model car, but this old Buick would be easier. I found the "odds and ends" aisle and grabbed a small over priced package of cheap speaker wire, then went to the front counter display cases and took an extremely cheap, poorly made, fake (convenience store) Swiss army knife.

Leaving the store with my bounty, I checked the area once again and approached the Buick. As I passed the other vehicle parked with its doors open, I was startled by a sound from inside...A squirrel was making itself a nice home, complete with nest in the back seat. I opened the door to the Buick and popped the hood. I followed the plug wires to the coil wire. I took the speaker wire, stripped both ends with the shitty Swiss army knife and ran it from the positive end of the battery to the positive side of the coil. This would supply power to the dash. The car would be useless without this.

I had to locate the starter solenoid. It was logically found on the starter. Using the longer knife blade on the knife, I completed the connection between the starter solenoid and the positive battery lead. There was a spark. The engine cranked over, then came to life. I would hard wire it later. The noise would surely attract them, so I had to hurry.

I took off my pack, and weapon and sat them in the passenger seat. Using the flathead screwdriver part of the knife, I was able to push the steering wheel locking pin away from the wheel to unlock it. I then tightened the speaker wire so that it wouldn't come off during the drive. I closed the hood, got in and then rolled the fucking windows up fast enough to break the sound barrier and headed for the road with a quickness. My lucky day, the poor bastard that owned the car actually filled the tank up before he presumably died. Looking at my map, my route was distinct.

I was on highway 185 northwest out of Seadrift, straight shot into Victoria. The road was far from being a major thoroughfare, so I had no trouble getting to the outskirts of Victoria in less than two hours. I was delayed by the occasional car parked sideways in the road, or an unusually large pack of creatures shambling across like sheep. As I approached the outskirts, I could tell that I was closer to a fall out area, as there was a light coat of ash on most horizontal surfaces, i.e. parked cars, houses and buildings. I am no expert on radiation, but I did see birds and small animals, so I took a chance in assuming it was semi-safe to at least transit the area.

Right now it's nearly 2030 hrs and I have been trying to hail the Grisham's on the radio for the past thirty minutes, No answer. This trip could have been a complete waste. Coming into town, I had to avoid being seen by a group of those monsters. I parked the car within short walking distance of the local Victoria, TX water tower. No sooner than I was three hundred yards away from my car, there were scores of them surrounding it. I have no idea how they can triangulate sounds like they do. A living person would be hard pressed to do this. My thoughts drifted to the structure of the ear, and how the parts must stiffen in death.

The sun will be setting soon, and I'm getting tired of writing. I am safely one hundred and fifty feet off the ground, on the tower with my pack. It is drizzling rain and I am miserable. I will continue to attempt contact with the survivors.

February 28th

0923 hrs

I found them. Not much time to write. I turned the radio on this morning at 0800 hrs, and walked around to the opposite side of the tower, just to make sure on reception. After three attempts, William's familiar voice answered up, "Thank god, we need help, where are you?" I exchanged information with him and told him that I have been picking up his transmission for a few days and that myself and another man named John were holding up at a marina on an island off the coast of Texas.

I asked him how things were and he said that his position was completely surrounded by the dead. I told him that I was broadcasting from the Victoria water tower and asked him where he was in reference to the tower. The directions he gave were simple, as he was only a couple miles from my location. Leaving now...

Left on Main. (Brown Ave.)
1/4 mile. Right on Elm. Keep going.
I'll know the house when I see it.

1641 hrs

I have them. William is driving.

After speaking with William this morning, I departed the area to look for them. I hot-wired the car again (much more simple this time) and sped toward the directions that I jotted down. The house was not difficult to find, as it was the one swarming with at least a hundred undead. I could see William's face through the gaping hole where the attic vent once was. Even from this distance, I could see the defeat in his eyes. I don't know what came over me. Maybe I am still human inside after all. There just might be a conscience there. I radioed William to "hang tight." I slammed on my brakes, jumped out of the car and opened fire on the crowd of devils. A hundred sets of white eyes immediately turned my way, and I could swear, one hundred mouths opened in unison and called my name.

Of course, my fear was making my eyes see this, but they were coming after me. I jumped back in the car, slammed it in reverse and turned around. Just when the first of them reached the car and started to pound, I took off leading them away from William and his family.

I keyed the microphone and told William to get his family ready to get out onto the roof as near to the ledge as possible. I was going very slowly, so that they would give chase and stay with me. William told me over the CB that they were all following me and that the plan was working. The only ones left behind, were the ones I was lucky enough to put down with a random freak headshot when I opened fire.

Rounding the block, I waited until they were almost upon me until I hit the fucking gas and made for the Grisham house. I could see William, his wife, and a little girl on the roof. I drove the car up to the side of the house to lessen the distance they would have to jump. I got out and covered them as William jumped first and held his arms out for the others.

One of them came walking outside the shattered front door, and saw William's wife as she was sliding down the roof, legs hanging over. It made for her. I took aim and popped the bastard in the mouth. That didn't stop it. I was getting tired. One more round to the dome put it in its place.

I swung my upper body back around to the street like a tank turret. Still clear. They were all on the ground. William started to say thanks when I cut him off. The two girls were in the back. William got in and put his seatbelt on. I passed my rifle to William and sped off, back toward Seadrift. It is going to be too dark to take the boat back to Matagorda. I have no way to find it in the dark, as I left the NVGs with John. We are going to have to find a safe place to sleep in or near Seadrift tonight.

February 29th

0645 hrs

I could not get John on the radio last night or this morning. We ended up sleeping on the boat. I pulled her out a hundred meters from the marina and anchored her. We were safe, and I actually got some decent sleep. The Buick is parked right next to the dock. Not sure if I will ever need it again, but it is a good car. Leaving in a few minutes for the island with the new survivors. Have not had much time to chat with them, as they slept very deeply as soon as we were safely anchored. The little girl (Laura) whined in her sleep last night.

0900 hrs

No sign of John. No note written, nothing. No sign of struggle. Myself, William, Jan, and little Laura are safe within the confines of the marina. I am worried about John. He is much too conservative to do something like this. Annabelle was happy to see me, but she was especially happy to see Laura. The little girl smiled and was very happy to have a dog to play with. Maybe John took a boat out and will show soon...

Stand

March 1st

1522 hrs

There is still no sign of John. I feel like I need to look for him, but I have no idea where to start. What would make him leave with no notice? His weapon is gone and the drawbridge mechanism we rigged is drawn back. It is all very confusing. I am taking this down time to get to know the Grisham family a bit better. They do not know John, but can see the worry in my eyes that I am trying to hide.

March 3rd

0914 hrs

John was bloody, tired and defeated. He came back this morning and called out to me. I ran outside and pushed the marina drawbridge over to him. He fainted at the shoreline and I had to carry him inside. John isn't a big man, only about 160 lbs. I slung him over my shoulder and walked over the drawbridge, and pulled the rope to slide it back my direction and attach it back to the marina wall. When I got him inside and put him on a makeshift bed, I noticed the photograph in his bloody hand.

A bloodstained picture of a woman fell to the floor from his clutch. I knew in my heart who it was. It was his wife. He has been in and out of consciousness since his arrival early this morning. He has taken some water, and has attempted to drink some canned soup. Janet and I will continue to monitor him.

William's wife, Jan was a registered nurse (quit her nursing job a couple years ago for medical school). She wasn't a doctor, but who is anymore?

Janet examined him head to toe, paying special attention to John's lacerations. None of them appeared to be bite marks. One of them looked like a small caliber bullet wound (entry and exit wound on his shoulder), while others looked like tumble injuries. John was in no shape to explain anything as he could barely take a drink of water/soup without vomiting and passing out. I am worried.

March 4th

2014 hrs

John finally snapped out of it. I told him how worried I was, and how I had no idea what happened to him. He then proceeded to tell me that he hit his breaking point during the loneliness of the past few days. While I was away, all he could think of was his wife and son, and how much he loved them. Jan was listening from the adjacent room, and I could tell she felt for him. John told me how he remembered leaving some items in the aircraft when we abandoned it, and he was missing the only picture he had of his wife. He told me that he could never ask me to risk my life over a picture, so instead of waiting on me to get back, he decided that he would attempt to get it on his own.

He made it to the ruined aircraft, and retrieved the small bag containing the photo, and immediately started heading back. He was soon besieged by many undead, and had to take refuge in a hotel. He managed to barricade the second floor of the five-floor hotel. He then proceeded to clear out any unsecured guests with his .22 rifle. After three days and nights of enduring the sounds of the trapped undead guests in their rooms, he decided to make an escape.

He went room to room (ensuring they were not occupied) and collected sheets from the vacant beds. Using square knots, he formed a long escape rope. Early on the morning of his escape, he found the right window to climb out of. The window he chose was on the third floor, and a large tree growing near the window obscured street view. He climbed down the sheets with his rifle slung over his shoulder. He dropped the non-breakable gear to the ground.

About the time he started climbing down, he felt one of the knots starting to slip on his sheet rope. It was too late to climb back up and check. He continued his descent. The knot gave way as he reached the 2nd floor level. He fell hard and fast through the tree branches and was cut up pretty well on the way down. When he hit the ground, his rifle discharged and the bullet entered the back of his shoulder and exited the front.

His next memory was of me carrying him back onto the dock.

March 5th

1230 hrs

Woke up this morning in a cold sweat around 0600. The Grisham family was still sleeping in the other room of the marina. John and I were crashed out on the two couches in the office. I know I had a terrible dream last night, but I just can't grasp what it was. I just remember running...fast. The first thing I saw when I woke up, were the small droplets of blood on the wall, left over from the harbor-master's suicide. John didn't wake up until 1130 or so.

Thankfully, the bullet wound and lacerations don't seem to be critically infected, just some small reddening around the edges of some of the cuts. Lucky for him, the round passed through his shoulder. He might have died of infection if one of us had to attempt to extract it on our own.

Medical supplies would be a nice luxury to have, especially since there is someone around that might be able to use them. Of course, a nice bunker with eight-foot thick steel walls, geothermal power, and unlimited food and water would be nice also. People in hell want ice water.

...Who am I kidding?

There is no more hell.

Hell is here.

I want ice water.

Quiet Time

1944 hrs

Laura and Annabelle played in the back room of the marina while Jan, John, William and myself talked about our experiences. William explained his situation in the attic, and how it came to that. John was lying on the couch with his make shift sling (ironically made from a torn sheet).

I expressed the fact that we can't exist here on this island forever. We would never be safe from the hordes that are roaming the streets. What if a hurricane came and washed the marina away, or even worse, washed it up on the shore? A million things could go wrong. We only have limited fuel here for the boats. None of us know how to fix/operate the large ferry docked next to us. I asked William why he had to be a chemist and not a boat mechanic. He apparently has a decent sense of humor for a chemist.

I inquired to Jan as to how Laura was taking all of this. Jan expressed that she was unusually resilient to all of the horror she had witnessed in the past couple months. I heard Laura whine in her sleep again last night, but did not mention this to Jan, as I am sure she is no stranger to this.

It must be my military nature, but I feel like we are in the same situation as John and I were in at the tower. I feel like we need to make plans, and need to make them fast. I cannot foresee any danger here at the marina, as we have our own little man made island, but again, John and I had a two hundred foot tower surrounded by a high chain link fence, and were under siege within minutes.

Maybe I am just paranoid.

We have our code words established for Laura when we see

one or more of those things outside. We play "quiet time." This lets Laura know that it is not time to play and jump and giggle with Annabelle. Today one of those things was shambling about, very near the shoreline where the floating walkway would be if it were connected to the shore. Its rotted body was having a difficult time raising its head, but it managed to look in my direction as I peered out the blinds at it. I know the thing is dumb and dead, but I still felt a calculating stare, as it kept looking over here. More came soon after. Some looked as if they died recently. These moved faster and more methodically than their rotted counterparts. I would definitely make it a point to avoid them with more zeal.

March 6th

0322 hrs

I woke up a half hour ago and cannot get back to sleep so I decided to check the shoreline with the night vision goggles. I see numerous figures walking around the area near the shoreline. I can hear a sound coming from the direction of the tall buildings. I can't quite figure out what it is. For some odd reason it sounds like a TV that is turned up too loud. This made me want to check our TV here, but I will wait until it is light outside so that the light from it cannot be seen on the shore. Why do they remain here? Do they sense us?

If I had a suppressed weapon, I would execute the lot of those miserable creatures right now.

1242 hrs

Brainstorming, brainstorming, brainstorming. I spent the whole morning thinking of possible safe areas. Of course, no place is truly safe. All of the heavily fortified buildings or prison facilities would be impenetrable, and useless without access. This island will not do. Maybe a smaller island, with less of an undead population. One would think that an island would be ideal in this situation but there is nowhere to run and the only supplies on the island are already here. Once we run out of the low hanging fruit type supplies that are easily scavenged from nearby buildings, that will be it. William told me of his neighbor and how he was bitten. He swore it didn't take more than a few hours for him to succumb to the wound and turn. It only takes one of them. I read somewhere that even the best thieves concede to the fact they will get caught eventually, it's just the law of averages.

Basing my chances of survival on this premise, I too feel that my day will come. All I can do is attempt to survive. I have never had any children and I see the worried look in William and Jan's eyes when Laura asks to go outside. That <u>is</u> shit for an existence. I feel somewhat responsible for everyone. I know that if any of them succumb to the dead, I will feel great sorrow. There must be a group of people somewhere. The question is, do I want to make myself known? I moved the harbor radio near John's couch so that he could monitor it. He enjoys this, and it gives him something to do while he recovers.

I still have my stolen state map of Texas. There aren't many details given about Matagorda Island, but there is a hospital a couple miles south of our position. John's wounds do not seem to be getting any worse, so I'm not sure I will even need to find any medication, but I suppose it's nice to know it's there if I want to risk my ass.

No broadcast on the TV. I could have sworn I heard something like it in the distance this morning. One station has a high-pitched ringing sound, but only snow for the picture. The radio station is still playing, and I think I have almost memorized the order of the songs, and all the commercials. Just a constant loop until the power goes out or the tape/digital feed fails. I wonder what kind of rotting filth is trapped in that DJ booth right now?

We are fast approaching spring and I don't like the idea of being at the mercy of a hurricane if one were to pop up here. I hate to keep moving, but it seems to be the only thing that has kept me alive.

March 7th

2123 hrs

When John and I visited Seadrift on our food gathering expedition, we put all we could into two shopping carts and got the hell out of there. That amount would have lasted us awhile with just us. Now, we have three more mouths to feed. John wasn't yet able to handle himself out there, so that leaves William. I approached him about it today. I sort of feel guilty, considering he has a wife and child. I couldn't go out there alone and expect to survive. I needed someone to at least be the eyes behind me while I work. He looked at me and told me that I didn't even need to ask, and then he went on to tell me how grateful he was. I don't take compliments or tributes too well so I just thanked him and changed the subject.

After conducting an inventory of food and water, my best guess is that we have enough food to last a week. Just reading that sounds like great news, for a complacent person. I would prefer to have one month plus a week for backup. William only has very limited experience with firearms. This would have to change for him to be effective out there. After discussing with William what would have to be done in the coming days, he agreed to let me teach him how to operate John's .22 rifle.

We checked the outside for any lurking corpses. We saw only one shambling parallel to our position, pre-occupied with something on the ground. I loaded my rifle as well as John's .22 and enough rounds to do what we set out to do. I left my pistols behind for Jan, ready to shoot. I explained to her that she not leave them where Laura could get them, and the basics of how to hold and aim the weapon. I knew they would be safe while William and I were away, and we would only be gone for an hour.

William and I quietly stepped onto the boat and untied her. We rowed in unison for fifteen minutes so that we would be clear of the marina area. This time, instead of heading toward Seadrift (west), we headed up the coast toward the more populated area of Matagorda Island. No better way to practice than with real targets.

I could tell that William was nervous. I told him to relax, and that we were not going to set foot on shore today. This relieved some of his tension and made things seem more pleasant. Twenty yards from shore, and very near three large beachfront hotels was where we anchored the Bahama Mama. I hated to do this to William, but better he sweat in training than bleed in battle. I started making noise and whistling and screaming out to them. It wasn't long before the beach was teaming with dozens of them. Some of them waded knee deep in the water before stumbling backward to dry land.

It was then I started teaching William how to load and fix a jammed weapon. I figured that if he could load while being taunted by the dead, he could do it anywhere. He fumbled and dropped a few rounds on the deck of the boat, but overall he picked up quickly how to load the weapon and aim it. I took the weapon from him and replaced the loaded magazine with the spare unloaded I had hidden in my pocket (without him seeing). He was gazing nervously at the shoreline when I handed the cocked weapon back to him and told him to aim at the creature in the red shirt.

Dramatically, I explained to him the basics of aiming and how he needed a head shot to kill them. Ideally I told him I wanted the shot to hit on the top 1/3 of the cranium. I told him to breath, long deep breaths...Only when he was ready, should he squeeze, then only on the exhale...

I was testing him. Would he anticipate the small kick of the .22 and yank the weapon when he depressed the trigger? I told him to take the shot...

With both eyes open, like I told him, he gazed through the sights and squeezed the trigger. CLICK...

William jerked high and to the right, his mental reflexes telling him to do so. He then looked over at me, confused. I told him what I had done and why. Over the next few minutes I would take the weapon and randomly load a round to test him. Soon he didn't jerk the weapon at all. His first kill was a direct hit, entering the eye of the lucky corpse destroying the brain as the shell bounced around in the rotting skull.

I loaded ten rounds into the magazine and told him to go to town, killing the fully mobile creatures first. Soon the shoreline was littered with nearly twenty still corpses. In total, this little shooting lesson used up twenty rounds. We still had almost 800 .22 rounds.

We pretty much drew every corpse within a ten-mile radius to our position. No matter, better to draw them here than back to the marina. I pulled anchor and sped farther up the coastline leading them further away from the marina. After five minutes of this I flipped her around and headed away from the island to mask the sound of our return. When we were reasonably close, we cut the engines and paddled back to the stronghold. I feel a little better about taking William with me now that he is more confident in himself.

March 9th

2047 hrs

Yesterday and today were interesting. My humanity bucket hadn't been filled for a while, and it was getting dry and rustic. After the marital spat John and I witnessed today, I know that this plague cannot and will not destroy human nature. Since there was no television, and taking nice walks through the city was not encouraged, this was my entertainment most of the morning.

It wasn't my nostalgia that they were fighting about, it was theirs, but the pre-apocalypse nature of the fight moved me. It was a simple fight over laundry and housework, and who actually did it around the house before all of this. It felt so good to hear a normal conversation for once, and not once hearing about how we were going to avoid one of those things biting our asses off.

Food: Not critical yet, but a revised estimate of (5) days remaining.

Laura wants to go outside and play, "Like her friends at school get to do." I tried to explain to her, with my limited "small people" knowledge that it wouldn't be any fun to play outside right now, and that the people out there wouldn't be nice. She looked at me and rolled her eyes and said, "I know they are dead, you don't have to play." I was shocked at the little girl's candor and just sort of chuckled under my breath.

I wondered which parent she took the attitude from. Using my knife I carved a chess board into the table in the lounge area of the marina. I stole some fishing lures from the marina retail area and John and I are utilizing them (sans the hooks) as chess pieces. So far I have him three games to two.

I have a strange feeling that William and Jan have made amends for the silly argument, as I can hear no loud voices through the other end of the privacy curtain I put up for them a few days ago.

Enemy activity: Sporadic movement. Last night's full moon brought hundreds of them near us. Using NVGs, I studied them. They seemed to be more active. Could this be because of the full moon? I doubt it.

I gave my last few sets of foam earplugs to the Grishams. Laura was fascinated at how they returned to their original shape after you squeezed them. John still had his set in his pant pockets.

I had no earplugs left, so I took two 9mm rounds out of the ammo box and stuffed them in my ear. They were a good fit and really drowned out their moans last night.

March 10th

1222 hrs

The radio station stopped playing music today. For a brief moment I heard a human voice on the other end. It sounded like I heard the word "fortify" before the microphone cut out. John and I were playing chess again when it happened. Now, I can't even pull John away from the CB radio. He keeps trying to broadcast in the hopes that whoever stopped the music will hear and respond. The station is broadcasting out of Corpus, so I know for a fact they are overrun. I also know that the radio John is using won't reach that far. Whatever keeps his spirits up, I suppose.

William and I spoke about his chemistry skills. I asked him if he could make anything useful, considering our current situation. He said that if he had the ingredients, he could make pretty much anything. With William being a chemist, and John being an engineer, I'm sure they can come up with something to help our current predicament.

Thought: I wonder what historical sites were destroyed that Laura will never see. I remember visiting the Alamo last year. I wonder if anyone alive was holding their ground in the true last stand of the Alamo when the warhead hit.

Maybe it answered a prayer...

March 12th

2145 hrs

→ Food: (2) days remaining.

→ Water: Still have pressure, however starting to taste funny. Will need purification tablets soon. If I develop any symptoms, i.e. diarrhea, I will have to find some purification tablets, or simply boil it.

William knows the time to leave is coming. Tomorrow we will have to head out for supplies or starve here. It is raining and the water is getting choppy, causing the marina to wobble just enough to induce discomfort. No signal on the formerly good radio station. I have been studying the map I procured last trip very closely. There are other options to scavenging. We could head northeast up the coast line and cherry pick, but run the risk of boat mechanical failure which would put us in a world of shit.

Another option is to go back to "old faithful" Seadrift.

Across San Antonio bay, on the western shoreline is another small town called Austwell. I figure we might as well check it out while we are gathering supplies, and food. I need extra batteries for the NVGs and some first aid supplies.

John is recovering nicely and almost has limited mobility of his arm. The lacerations are healing but without stitches, he will have to take it easy for a while. Jan used duct tape to dress the wounds and keep them closed. Yet another use for it. William promised Laura that he would bring her back something from our trip. I suppose it was customary when William went away on business, to bring his little girl something back. I will do my best to make sure that happens.

I really dread these outings, and wonder if there will ever be a time when I can walk freely again. I will continue making the shopping list tonight, and then, I will gas up the boat in the dark to avoid attention. I am going to try to be in the sack by midnight.

March 13th

0745 hrs

Ready to leave. The equipment is loaded onto the boat. It has stopped raining, and the water is not as choppy. Left my Walther P99 with John, and Jan. Not much firepower left behind for them, but I don't think they will need it. Our destination is Austwell, TX (Opposite side of San Antonio bay from Seadrift). Austwell is also a small dot on the map, hopefully indicating a small population of undead. This outing serves two purposes. One, to get William more comfortable with being among them so we can plan for a bigger picture. Secondly, to gather much needed supplies.

We now have six souls in our little marina island (including Annabelle), and with two people, I estimate we can only gather maybe a weeks worth of food at a time. This means that we are theoretically forced out into their world once a week, which in my opinion is one time too many. I need to step out of the box with my shopping. Yes, the junk food, soup cans, and other things we have been looting are great, but the lack of vitamins and exercise is catching up with me. My metabolism has slowed down from lack of being able to run.

Luck be with us.

2233 hrs

After leaving the marina and paddling out to "safe engine distance" we cranked it up and sped toward San Antonio bay. I could see birds in the air, and the smell of the open air was refreshing. Soon the Texas mainland was in plain view in front of us. Entering the bay was exactly like the two times before. After reaching the western shore, a few private docks could be seen. Up a small hill from each of them, stood a large house. I suppose the docks were for the owner's boats, although I could see none tied up.

We cut the engines and started our two-man rowing toward the shoreline. I sat and thought about how silly I would look to an onlooker if this had never happened. I closed my mind and continued to row, imagining that everything was normal.

It was a complete mess. Windows were shattered, rats, trash, newspapers, everything was blowing around the dock and street. There was large parking lot in the asphalt area beyond the marina ramp. I could see five creatures surrounding a white compact car, and beating their rotting hands on the windows. I could not see inside of the car from this distance and angle. I assumed that there was definitely something in the car that the creatures were after, and an even further assumption would be that it was alive, whatever it was.

Quietly, we rowed to the tie up point and docked the boat. I slung my empty pack on my back, put the pry bar in my belt, put some heavy plastic zip ties in my pocket and readied my weapon, then stepped into this new world. I didn't look behind me, but I could feel William's presence there. I could almost smell his fear. I was probably more afraid than he was. Scanning the area, we crept across the ramp to the shore, eyes trained on the small white Ford that was surrounded by the dead. As soon as I set foot on terra firma, I grabbed a fist sized rock on the shore, threw it as hard as I could, about twenty meters beyond the car into the windshield of a large black truck. It sounded like someone beat a snare drum when the rock hit home. The things instantly stood erect and started walking toward the area beyond the car.

I told John to stay back and watch for them while I checked things out. I was almost on top of it. The car was an arms length away. I reached out to touch the hood, feeling its cold surface. I could see a figure with the seat down, lying in the driver's seat. It was an attractive woman that looked in her early twenties. The car windows were caked with dried rot, and puss from the creature's relentless pounding. Most of the windows were cracked in a spider web pattern.

I put my face up to the window to get a closer look at the woman. She looked dead. I could see signs of extreme dehydration in her face. Her lips were dry and flaky. The creatures that were gathered here, were now preoccupied elsewhere. I called William over. I asked him how long it took for one to turn (I remember him telling me he had witnessed this before). He said that he had seen a man die in the street, as he watched from the attic of his home, and he turned within the hour.

Nothing made sense. There was an open bottle of aspirin spilled out onto the passenger seat, and empty plastic water bottles strewn all over the car. She couldn't have been dead longer than a day. I suppose the question I was asking myself was, why didn't she turn like the others?

In the back seat, I could see numerous fast food beverage cups, filled with what looked like feces and urine. She had been trapped in this car for what looked like a few days.

Then there was movement. First her mouth gestured a weak yawn, and then her eyes started to flutter. I trained my weapon on her and told William to watch my back and keep a lookout in the immediate area. Expecting to see the familiar milky death orbs staring at me, I was surprised when she opened her eyes, and I could see the blue in her irises. She looked up at me in shock. To her, I was a strange man, wearing a mask, with a machine gun pointed at her. She looked behind her and around the car and with her lips only, said with no voice, "I'm alive."

I pulled off my mask and went to the door to open it. It was locked. She smiled and looked at me, and unlocked it. I took her arm and helped her out of the car. She stank worse than those things. Maybe it was the car. I had to support her as she walked. She was very weak and sore from being trapped in the car. Looking over my shoulder, I motioned William to follow me back to the boat.

After reaching the Bahama Mama, I sat her down, gave her some water and some canned beef (my lunch). I told her not to eat or drink anything too fast. I didn't have time to stay and chat. William had his instructions. He was to row the boat out twenty meters and drop anchor and wait for me. I was going shopping.

As I stepped back onto the dock, I could hear William rowing the boat away from me. I reached the parking lot again, and I could see more than five in the area. I stayed low and followed the shoreline toward the town. No sign of life anywhere. No dog, cat, nothing. I didn't even see any birds flying over this town. I was coming up on a group of buildings. I cut inland and walked toward what was the center of the small town of Austwell, Texas. After a few hundred meters of walking, I stepped through a clearing. I could see a Walgreen's and a gas station.

I doubt Walgreen's had any food, but I was certain they had medical supplies. I crept up to the front door, sticking to the wall. This door was different in the way that it actually had chains holding the doors shut from the inside. There would be no way for me to get in without busting the glass, and attracting them. I walked to the back of the store. There was a drive up window for the pharmacy there. That side of the building faced the woods. There could be hundreds of them in there looking at me and I wouldn't know it. I couldn't feel them, but then again, I wonder if that sense still exists when it comes to their kind.

There was a steel exterior cargo shutter door, probably for new shipments. Tried to lift it up. Locked tight. I really need to get a book on lock picking from the local library. Pulled out the bar from my belt. I placed the bar under the shutter underneath the keyhole. After a few minutes of prying, cursing, and sweating, I finally broke the lock. I checked my surroundings, noticing that I had garnered some unwanted attention one block away and closing.

I attached my LED light to my carbine and twisted it on. It was dark in the cargo area as it was separate from the sky lit main retail part of the store. I shined the light into the room. I could only see boxes, steel shelves and various other normal things. I jumped up into the loading bay. Just as I started to slide the shutter door down, two of them rounded the corner and caught sight of me. I slammed the garage door type shutter down and immediately thought of a way to secure it. I held the shutter down with the bottom of my boot just as the first creature started beating on the metal. They would attract more. The plastic zip ties in my pocket would do no good, as I had nothing on the ground to secure the door to. I glanced over to the corner of the room where I found a mop and some nylon string. Walking over the corner, I kept my right foot along the lip of the door, and my left for balance. Grabbing the mop, I wedged it between the rollers that made the door slide up smoothly. Using the twine, I secured it in place. There was a heavy box on the shelf full of plastic bottles of mouthwash. I sat the box on the lip of the door where my foot was. This wouldn't work forever, but it would have to work for now.

After I was satisfied that the door would hold for at least a little while, I stepped into the pharmacy. Numerous pharmaceutical books lined the shelves. Picking up the Physicians Desk Reference, I scanned it for any possible useful information regarding medication. I would love to take this back to Jan, but it was a rather large book and would take up valuable backpack space.

There was another book listing numerous antibiotics. Using this book, I grabbed bags of pills left in the pick-up bin that would never be claimed. Basically anything with a "biotic" on the end of it found its home in the plastic zip lock bag in my pack. Jumping over the counter, I landed on the main floor and immediately pointed my weapon toward a blind spot of the store.

Looking up, I noticed that this store had convex observation mirrors, enabling easy view of most of the area. I checked the mirrors, and cleared the store, row by row. The creatures were still steadily banging on the back shutter door. I hated this. I felt rushed. Tylenol, hydrogen peroxide, bandages, band-aids, I stuffed them all in the big zip lock freezer back with the antibiotics. I saw some iodine on the shelf and remembered in Navy survival school that iodine worked as a water purifier. I tossed it in the pack. I was thirsty. I grabbed a warm bottle of water off the shelf and downed it. My pack was half way full. I passed the candy bar section and grabbed a chocolate bar.

Opening it, I realized how long it had been since all of this started. The bar was long stale. No matter, I needed energy. On the toy aisle, I found a small teddy bear, and put it in the pack. After eating the candy, I started looking for my escape.

I was at the main entrance doors. The chain was a standard, heavy steel chain. I didn't want to walk in front of the doors, in case I had to use this way as a way out. There was no way I would get that heavy steel Master lock off without either shooting the hell out of it, or hitting it a hundred times with a fire axe. I grabbed some duct tape off the store shelf. Quietly, (not that it mattered over the sound of the creatures in the back slamming against the metal shutter) I taped up the bottom section of the glass door, making sure that I was not seen.

It took a few minutes but soon the whole section was covered. Then, using the fire extinguisher from behind the counter, I bashed it outward. It wasn't as loud as it could have been, but still too loud for me. Quickly, I headed back the way I came, through the wooded area toward the marina parking lot. I had been gone for over an hour. I ran through the woods. I was nearly sprinting. I could see the clearing ahead of me.

There were two of them in the woods in front of me. I juked them and kept running. When I hit the clearing, my heart stopped. There were so many of them. I skirted the parking lot, avoiding attention. I had no choice but to make myself known. I ran out toward the dock and I knew that they saw me. Their orchestrated moans bounced off the water and echoed from all directions nearly demoralizing me into the fetal position.

I was in flight mode. I called out to William. No sight of the boat. I kept running. —Still no boat. Looking back, I could see them all converging on the dock. No way out. I had ten feet of dock left and the things were twenty feet from my position. They were so hungry. They were rotted, putrid evil. In their frenzy, they knocked their fellow demons into the water... —just to be the first to eat my flesh. I turned and ran.

I dove into the water and started swimming away. I did the sidestroke for a full minute before I started treading water and looking back toward the dock. The dock was full of bodies, so full that many fell off from lack of standing room. There I was, treading water, alone. I kept imagining that there was something below the water tugging on my boots. I was terrified and accidentally swallowed some water down the wrong pipe and imagined how many of those things were rotting in the murky deep.

Then came the hum of an engine. I still had all my gear strapped to my body, but it is surprising how easy it is to float if you just blow some air into your clothing. I waved excitedly at the boat. It was William. He saw me.

The boat went to idle and drifted over to my position with the engine still running. I handed William my pack and my rifle from the water. I then pulled myself on board. William told me that the parking lot filled shortly after I left. He had no choice but to try and drive them away from the marina for my safety. I checked my backpack; only a little water seeped into the freezer bags. Not enough to hurt the contents.

We headed back to John, Jan, Laura, and Annabelle. I was wet, cold and without the food I set out to get. If the boat had not shown, I don't know where I would have ended up. I'm not sure how long I could have swam and would have undoubtedly been followed down the shoreline until I was too tired to swim any longer. Admitting defeat, my tired body would have been torn apart as I stumbled into the shallows... —Into open arms.

Ides of March

March 15th

1822 hrs

I spent yesterday and today fighting off a cold from my recent swimming adventure and also cleaning and drying my rifle. Only in a world like this could a common cold mean a death sentence. It's not bad, I just feel weaker than normal and a little fever. Jan advises against using any antibiotics unless in dire need, as she claims the body would get used to the medication and it would do no good in the future if really needed. Jan also tended to the new arrival, Tara. Tara had been trapped in that car for days. She was on the verge of dying from dehydration when William and I showed up. She was feeling better. Tara had made sure she stayed hydrated and in bed.

I caught her looking at me a few times today. She didn't catch me, but I did the same. She was attractive, and I am human. I overheard her conversation with Jan about how she got to the dock.

Trapped in her house in Austwell, she saw an opportunity for escape. She made it to the marina and was spotted by three of them while looking for a boat to escape in. She had no choice but to seek shelter in the nearest unlocked car she could find. Tara was a marketing major at a local junior college. She commented on how none of it mattered and figured that her marketing career was now over before it started. Both women laughed at this.

William and John took the boat out and caught ten fish yesterday. John was up to it and I figured some sun would do him good. Laura asked me how my trip to the store went. I told her it went fine, and that I was sorry I didn't find her anything to eat. She said it was ok and that her daddy didn't bring her anything back from the trip anyway. I remembered the bear. I gave it to William so he could sun dry it before giving it to her, as it got wet when I jumped in the water to escape the creatures. I told Laura not to be sad and that he had a present for her and he was just waiting for the right time to give it to her. She smiled and walked off to investigate.

Raw fish isn't my favorite entrée, but millions of Japanese can't be wrong. Well, maybe there are a million of them left alive, I wouldn't know. Once again, my personal groundhog day is coming and I dread leaving again. We need a better life, and a better place to live.

March 17th
1833 hrs

Around the table we were, like knights of old, discussing our battle plans. Jan, Tara, John, William and myself discussed at length all possibilities for finding a new place to live. An island strong hold has a certain mystique and attraction, however we ruled this out due to the constant need to travel to the mainland and scavenge. Where would a defensible position exist that was not near a major city?

There was a large map of the United States on the wall in the gift shop. It had no detail, just rivers and state lines and capital cities. I pulled the map off the wall, and we all studied it at length. My own selfish reasons kicked in, and I suggested we take a boat along the coastline and cruise up the Mississippi river to find a suitable location (would be nearer to my parents). That was one option. William suggested we go by land to avoid the catastrophic effect of boat mechanical failure. John suggested sailing along the coast around southern Florida, and straight to the Bahamas.

Everyone smiled at that idea, but it goes back to having a limited supply of goods and the need to scavenge. We were safe for now, as all the noise our boat engine has been making on our fishing/scavenging trips has been fooling them to other parts of the island, but this wouldn't last forever. We needed a more permanent place to live.

We are all playing poker tonight as a morale booster. Lara, Annabelle, and "tubby" the teddy bear have other plans, they are playing house.

Refulgence of Claudia

March 18th

2148 hrs

We have been living off of fish the past few days. I found a propane cooking plate on one of the larger boats in the marina, and finally had some cooked meat. We have different food now. I ventured out on the island today with William. We took the Bahama Mama out west along the island coast to find some food. According to my map, Matagorda island is roughly 25 miles long and two to three miles wide. I thought about rigging a sound device up by remote as a distracter for these things, as to draw them to a certain point on the island while William and I explore other parts. John is working on the idea.

William and I found something of interest today. We must have went ten miles west along the coast when something appeared inland behind some trees. It looked like some sort of tower. When we got closer, it became apparent that this was the island's lighthouse. It was a large black spire rising up roughly one hundred and fifty feet with a large glass lens room at the top. At the base of the lighthouse stood the keepers home I assume. This area seemed secluded, but I knew it wouldn't be longer than a couple hours before the sound of our engines would bring them to our general location.

We dropped anchor ten feet from dry land. I jumped out into the ankle high water. It was warm. This area was more rural than the marina area. The upside to this is, less living population = less dead population. The downside was that the trees were blocking my view to most of the area around the lighthouse.

William had gotten better with the .22 rifle the past few days. We were down to 700 .22 rounds for his weapon, and I only had 450 .223 rounds (a little target practice for me also). We crept up to the wooded area around the lighthouse. Something was making noise though. The closer we got to the structure, the louder the noise was. It was a constant, even interval banging noise, but still no visual sign of the undead. We were at the clearing. The lighthouse looked very old. I'm sure at one point its flat black paint was glossy, but years of salt air and rain have made their mark. The house attached to the bottom of the lighthouse seemed more modern. Three months worth of weeds and grass grew in the yard. The banging noise was obviously coming from the direction of the lighthouse.

We moved in. I kept signaling him to check our flank, as to avoid a possible rear assault. —Bang...Bang...Bang... The noise kept on, similar to the timing of a second hand on a clock. William and I walked the perimeter of the lighthouse/house. It was obvious the direction the noise was coming from. The basement access door on the backside of the house was shaking with every pound made below. I wasn't a hundred percent sure, but I knew what was down there.

I knew the door was secure (for some odd reason from the outside) and whatever was down there would stay down there until the door rotted of the hinges, or I let it out. We approached the front door to the house. It was not locked but the windows were boarded up, which for the life of me I couldn't figure out. I carefully turned the knob and flung the door open and both of us jumped back, aiming our weapons. We must have looked ridiculous.

The house smelled of rotting flesh. Not good. I almost wanted to say "fuck it" and just live off of fish for the rest of my life, but I was here, and we all needed food and supplies. The floor of this seaside dwelling was old and wooden. Every creek sounded like thunder. We were in the living room. I whispered to William, "Do you think there is a door to the basement inside the house?" He wasn't sure. I hoped there wasn't. On the floor I immediately noticed dried blood. It led to the hallway. Bloody handprints were apparent, and looked as if someone or something dragged itself into the hallway.

I went first, and William followed. Rounding the corner to the hall, I noticed that the blood trail curved into what I thought was a bedroom. I followed it. Heart pounding, sweating, scared. I was at the door where the trail led. The door was shut, and dried bloody handprints were all over the bottom half of it. I listened and reached for the knob. No sound. I quietly turned the knob and opened the door an inch, and rot hit my nostrils. I could see a pair of legs clothed in dirty jeans lying on the bed. I walked in. I saw what was left of a man, I think. His plaid shirt and denim were caked with blood, and his head from the nose up was gone. Maggots infested the open wounds, and I could see his skin move from the crawling larva underneath.

A twelve gauge hunting shotgun sat on his chest. Pulling the shotgun from his rotting grip, I noticed a yellow piece of paper with writing in black ink.

Feb. 12th

My dearest Claudia,

I love you so much. I know you are in heaven looking down, + you know the pain I am feeling. Even though I know that it is not you in the basement, still, I cannot bring myself to do it.

Please forgive me for not giving you peace.

I am a coward.

May God forgive me for what I am about to do.

I will always love you.

—Frank

I handed the note to William. None of us spoke for the next few minutes. The shotgun was a nice find, and so were the three boxes of shells on the dresser. We checked inside the dresser, in the sock drawer and found a .357 Smith and Wesson revolver with a box of fifty shells. Next was the kitchen. The canned goods, cooking oil and spices and anything else non-perishable were coming with us. There wasn't as much food as I expected to find. The incessant banging kept on relentlessly. Claudia wasn't giving up.

I remembered seeing a wheelbarrow around back near the basement door. I took it to the front and William and I filled it with our findings. I told William my thoughts about the basement, and that there may be more food and weapons down there. We agreed to open the door and take care of Claudia.

William volunteered to open the door and let me shoot. Carefully, he slid the "t-handle" lock up, out of the concrete sleeve, unlocking the door. The banging continued. She didn't know we were here, she just knew she was hungry and wanted out. I dreaded the thought of looking at her.

William grabbed the handle and was about to pull when I told him to wait. There was a safer way. I told William to find some rope or twine in the house. After a few minutes, he came back with a ball of knitting yarn from one of the spare bedrooms. I had him double it up and tie it to the handle and step back fifteen or so feet. I gave him the signal, and he yanked the doubled up yarn, pulling the door open.

There she was...rotted, putrid, evil. Her rotting milky eyes locked onto us and what was left of her lips curled back over her yellow, jagged teeth. Her hands were nothing more than bloody nubs from countless weeks of impact with the wooden cellar door. She lunged for us. Just as she reached the outside of the doorway, she tripped over the top step and tumbled face first into the ground. I took this opportunity to give her the peace that Frank could not. I shot the back of her head at point blank range, sending her back to her husband.

The cellar was dark and foreboding. I switched on the flashlight mounted on my rifle. The bright LED light filled the stairwell. Giving my eyes a moment to adjust, I thought about what other horrors could or would be lurking down here in the bowels of this old lighthouse. I stepped down into the darkness and found no creatures, living or dead. Claudia was it. I called William down to help. There were countless mason jars filled with green beans, yams, and other vegetables. There was also a considerable wine selection, and more canned goods.

It looked as if Frank and Claudia originally held up down here, as a bed, stove and refrigerator were in place and a Remington 7mm mag. hunting rifle with a scope sat barrel up, propped in the corner. On top of the refrigerator, were two boxes of 7mm shells. We took as much food as we could carry, along with the hunting rifle.

We filled our packs with the food, weapons and ammunition. The majority of the goods we found went in the wheelbarrow. I took off my pack and told William I would be back shortly. I walked toward the lighthouse. I wanted to go to the top to get a better view and see if we could expect any company. Round and round I went up the spiral staircase to the apex of the spire.

Reaching the top, I scanned the area. In the direction we came from, (east) I could see maybe twenty of those things milling about in a group headed our general direction. The sound of our boat and the gunshot were the catalysts.

I judged by their current rate of movement that we had plenty of time to leave. I ran back down the stairs and William and I took turns pushing the wheelbarrow back to the boat. We loaded up the Mama and headed back home. We got lucky today.

March 20th

1517 hrs

I just received a radio broadcast over the Citizen Band radio. The person claimed to be a congressman from the state of Louisiana, safe in a bunker a hundred miles north of New Orleans. His voice was rugged and tired. He went on to claim that he had many surviving soldiers of the Louisiana National Guard with him. The reason for his announcement was to warn any possible survivors of the threats posed by the radiation exposed undead. Apparently, New Orleans was destroyed in the strategic nuclear bombing campaign.

The congressman had sent out scouts equipped with dosimeters and Geiger counters to survey the damage to the city and the undead ranks. Out of the ten sent out, six returned. The scouts reported to the congressman that the radiation riddled undead showed little signs of decomposition and were faster and more coordinated than their non-irradiated counterparts. The radiation was somehow preserving them. One of the soldiers even claimed that they thought they heard one of the creatures speak a simple word. Of the four scouts that were killed two of them died from being overran by a dozen radiated undead on the interstate outside of New Orleans. The other two died from radiation exposure because they unknow-ingly spent the night in a fire truck drenched with radiation as the other scouts slept safely in a concrete drainage pipe five feet underground.

The congressman claims to have limited high-frequency teletype communications with a base equipped with squadrons of prototype UAVs and warehouses full of high-ordnance military explosives.

According to the broadcast, EMP burst has rendered much of the non-shielded electronics around the devastated city useless. The scouts had no luck hotwiring cars or finding salvageable radio equipment. This is something that I will file into the back of my mind for future reference in the event my luck is bad enough to find myself inside the blast radius aftermath.

John tried to respond to the transmission, however our low power transmitter didn't have the juice to make it that far. Maybe on a low overcast, cloudy day... —But not today. Just another thing to worry about.

March 22nd

1854 hrs

Tara is an interesting woman. I have to hand it to her for surviving. I can't begin to imagine her feelings of defeat as she sat in that compact car, and listened to them beat the glass for days. She told me that she spent one whole day attracting them to one side of the car, so that she could crack the window on the opposite side for a few precious seconds of cool air before they shambled back over. I haven't seen her break down and cry yet, but it is a natural thing, and I'm sure it will come.

Laura is in her own little world with Annabelle and her teddy bear. I have feelings of dread for the day that will come soon, the day we must move on. I somehow feel like I am responsible for everyone here. It would be too much to bear to lose any of them, however I know that sooner or later statistics will catch up with us. I have become decently good at chess and John and I are about fifty-fifty when we play.

William woke up last night at around 0200. I was awake looking at the map. He told me that he dreamed of our lighthouse trip and that the woman in the cellar, "Claudia" didn't trip in his dream. I thought about what he was getting at and just tried to put it out of my mind. I haven't seen any of them since our trip. We have been successful in confusing them with our boat/gunshot noise diversions.

No transmissions from Louisiana today or yesterday. We have been vigilant in having at least one person within earshot of the radio at all times. I have been in a slump since the lighthouse, so I decided to shave today for morale. Amazing how the feel of a good shave can make you feel more human.

I have been thinking about how many of them there are. I wonder just how outnumbered we are and just how much of the professional military was left. I remember the last US census back in 2000 and how they claimed there were close to three hundred million people in the US. I have no way of knowing how many survivors there are, but I am certain that they outnumber us. I would say that the nuclear campaign cleared out a few million (including the living). I suppose I just don't have enough data for any kind of accurate estimate.

Drizzling rain dominates the visibility. Spring is coming and so are the storms.

March 23rd

1819 hrs

We received another transmission from Louisiana. This time, it was very garbled. The voice on the other end claims that all communications with NORAD have ceased. The theory they are posing is that it probably fell from the inside. They are trying to hack a video feed from their command center north of New Orleans, however attempts to do so have proven unsuccessful.

John is still drawing up some rough plans for a "distracter" to be used against the creatures. I also asked him to start thinking about a mobile way to charge dead batteries, as I feel that many of the car batteries on the mainland would be as dead as their owners. We are building the groundwork for escape and evasion. To where is not yet certain.

March 24th

2339 hrs

We have not been affected by radiation fallout. We should avoid the former major cities, as I'm sure deadly amounts of radiation will exist there as evident from the reports of the dead scouts. There is also the matter of the other information received a few days ago from Louisiana. I can hear them moaning. The wind is carrying it and it feels like they are right outside the window. I know this is not the case, but the thought of it is very disturbing. It is not a human moan. It sounds like a deep throaty sound, low and unnatural. I need to check the perimeter.

March 26th

2003 hrs

The creatures cannot swim, however they can "exist" in the water. It was clear outside today and the water was calm. We decided to go outside on the docks to get some sun. I brought my rifle in an attempt to make sure everyone was safe on our outing. Little Laura was looking pale from lack of sun and I just felt guilty that she never got any outside time. I stood, facing the shore as the others took off their shoes and let their feet dangle over the edge of the dock, into the water.

As I scanned the shoreline, I saw no movement, vice the tormented creatures that were trapped in the hotel room across the street from our location. I checked back over my shoulder and they seemed to be enjoying themselves. They were being quiet, and conscious of the dangers that lurked in the urban area around us. I looked down into the water and noticed something dark moving about under the surface. The dark green seawater restricted my visibility.

I called John over, and told William to stay and watch the others, and to tell them to get their feet out of the water. On the wall of the marina was a round foam life preserver, similar to the ones seen on ships, and a lifeguard hook for grabbing people out of the water. I glanced at the hook and glanced at John. He brought it over to me as I continued to gaze into the green abyss. I saw it again. Something large was definitely moving under the surface.

I had John grab my belt and hold me solid as I dipped the long hook into the water. I felt it hit the object. After a few minutes of pulling and tugging, I finally snagged it. As I pulled the rotting thing up through the deep, I lamented over all the fish we had eaten in the weeks prior that had probably fed on this man's body. It was flailing and the mouth gaped and gnashed. As it opened its mouth in an attempt to take a bite out of me, I saw stagnant water pour out of the thing's throat and a low gurgle ensued.

It had no eyes, as they had surely been eaten by fish weeks before. This thing had been in the water a long time. I pulled it up onto the dock. As the torso cleared the water, it was apparent that the thing had no legs either. It was still dangerous so I decided to quietly dispatch it with a careful knife stab through the left eye socket. Using the hook bar, I held the head still as I carefully slid the knife home, neutralizing the pitiful fuck.

It would be a long time before I ever decided to take a leisurely swim in any body of water. I slid the dock bridge over to the land using the rope pulley. With the hook pole, I dragged the creature across the street as John covered me with his rifle. Laura saw the creature as I dragged the body away and started crying. I felt bad and hated the thing even more as I dragged the putrid mass across the ground. The corpse left a black stain on the concrete as the slimy torso grinded along the sun baked pavement.

March 27th

1951 hrs

Wind is howling outside. The moans of the creatures seem to be getting louder as the days go by. There are a couple dozen outside the marina "patrolling" the shoreline. Every second they are out there I have to tell myself not to go outside and execute them. There will be 9mm rounds stuck in my ear again tonight, because the noise is maddening. Even in the darkness of the new nightfall, I can still make out the drag marks on the shore from the corpse I neutralized yesterday.

We have agreed it is time to move. We set a target date of one week. In the meantime, we will be gathering more supplies and thinking of a suitable location. I have come to realize that if you do not move, you die. Even then you do not die, you exist as them, which is worse.

Atlantis

March 28th

1300 hrs

We are in the boat. Early this morning at around 0200 hours, a glass cup that Laura had left on the bait counter the night before fell to the floor for no apparent reason. I immediately stood up on my feet, and felt as if I was drunk, and it became difficult to stand up. It felt I was walking up hill toward the broken glass on the floor. I flipped the light switch on, and called to John and William. They too felt disoriented and it finally dawned on me what was happening.

I had wondered what took Murphy's Law so long to happen. We were sinking. It stormed last night and rocked us around a bit. I suppose lack of maintenance, inspections, and the wrath of nature finally did the job. We woke the others up and I suggested to John and William that they start gathering supplies. I had no idea how long we had before the whole marina bait/gift shop went down. The imbalance of weight vs. buoyancy would eventually snap the lumber support and cause the whole building to sink.

I had no time to be quiet. I donned the NVGs and immediately began getting the Mama ready. The noise I was making, combined with the creaking, overstressed timber of the marina had drawn a crowd. Through the graininess of my optics, I could make out roughly twenty creatures. They were god-awful. I felt in my heart that if there was a hell, these things came from there and in my imagination I could feel their hot hellish breath all over me.

Even though I was almost sure they could not see in the dark, many of them were looking in my direction, attuned to the noise, cocking their heads like a confused dog to its master. Most were in intermediate stages of decomposition, and I could not see their eyes through the goggles, only black circles, which added to their ominous horror.

Jan, Tara, John, William, and myself formed a human assembly line as we passed supplies hand over hand to the boat. Only half an hour had went by and already one of the corners dipped almost two feet into the water, causing the opposite corner to hang out of the water a foot or so. This meant the structure was getting over stressed.

I put the muzzle on Annabelle, and carried her and Laura to the boat and sat them down. The creatures were voicing their demented sounds toward us. I whispered to Laura not to worry and her job was to hold Annabelle, and not let her leave the boat. I handed her the teddy bear and pecked her on the cheek.

We loaded the boat down to an almost dangerous load bearing weight. It was the lowest I had seen her since we started using it. I helped Jan and Tara into the boat, and told William to stay while John and I made one last late check-out hotel room sweep of the place to make sure we didn't leave invaluable items. Satisfied with our sweep we boarded the boat and I fired the engine up. If it were not for Laura, I would have fragged a few of them that instant, if not only but to make myself feel better.

As we pulled away from the marina, I thought back to the places we were forced to take refuge in the past. They seemed to be getting less accommodating every time we move. We are now sitting one mile off the coast of Texas approximately, engine shut off, drifting to conserve fuel.

2144 hrs

Decided to cruise northeast up the Texas coast toward Galveston. Something is wrong with the engine. It keeps flooding. When I finally get the engine started again, it dies five minutes later. All hope is looking to be lost. By my approximations we have gone roughly 75 miles up the coast. We are running low on gas as I can see the level approaching the floor of the bladder tank. Still, that is not the problem with the boat. I assume it's something to do with the engine, and that means we are either rowing this tub at one knot per hour, or we are going to end up on foot.

It just can't get any better than this.

March 29th

0605 hrs

Oh yes it can. After rowing for four hours last night, we finally made it to a suitable anchor area away from any dead. After catching only two hours of sleep, we had no choice but to take our chances on foot. Tara had expressed to me that she needed to use the restroom, and that after the little problem we had with the creature under the water, she didn't really wish to hang her ass over the side. I guess I can understand. We can't stay on this small boat indefinitely. We paddled the boat near enough to shore for me to see the sandy bottom. I hopped out, ankle deep in salt water and pulled the boat further into the shore. William was covering me with the lighthouse keeper's shotgun. We unloaded as much as we could carry to the shore. We should be near Freeport, though I can't be sure.

Something seemed somehow perilous and foolish with the idea of trekking across mainland Texas with a little girl. I know she is not mine, but for some reason I feel very protective over her. As we sat on the shore I expressed to the men that we should move in a defensive posture, keeping the females (including Annabelle) in the middle and the males on the ends. We are leaving now and must leave some of the mason jars full of vegetables behind, along with some drinking water. We can't carry all the weight. As we leave the shore, I will take one look back at the Bahama Mama and say my mental good bye, just as I would a high school car that I had owned for years.

1341 hrs

After five hours of marching northwest inland, we are taking a short lunch break. I feel so vulnerable compared to the safety of the marina. Enough of them could easily over power us. Over the course of the past few hours, we have crossed numerous two-lane highways and some four-lane. We are in rough country. Some of it ranch. I guess our position to be somewhere in the vicinity of Sweeny, TX, but I cannot tell for certain and I refuse to ask the local population for help. The cacti grow freely everywhere. I supposed I never noticed it before, as I never made a point to just take off on foot across random ranch land.

We crossed one of the highways earlier this morning around 1030, there was a large six car pile up about a hundred meters away from where we crossed, it looked like a fire truck was on the scene with the ladder extended into the air. I decided to check it out and see if anything was salvageable. Looking at the wreckage, I thought to myself that I really didn't want to risk driving on the highways due to all the pileups we may encounter along our route. I didn't want to be trapped and surrounded by them in anything short of a tank.

As I neared the wreck site, my mind started piecing together what happened. I motioned for the others to stay put. The enemy was nigh. On top of the mechanical extended fire truck ladder, a creature, hanging from a safety tether took notice of my presence. No telling how long it had been hanging there, like a wild animal in a steel trap. This undead public servant was probably a good man in his former life. The bright yellow fireman's clothing was still visible under all the dried blood. A United States flag was stitched on his left sleeve with the date "9-11-01" embroidered into the stars and stripes.

I wanted to send this thing away with one well aimed round, but I knew this was different. We didn't have the safety of the boat to our advantage. I would let it hang there. I walked around to the other side of the wreckage. I figure that this fireman was attacked and took refuge forty feet up, at the top of the ladder for no telling how long. There was a small bucket big enough for one man to sit in at the top. He probably turned into what he is now and inadvertently fell and was doomed to hang there the rest of his rotting existence, from his safety line. There were feces on the ground below the ladder suggesting he made his stand for probably a few days. My question was, his stand from what? Other than his misfortunate corpse, there was no sign of the undead for as far as I could see to both sides of the wreckage. The bloody handprints at the base of the white mechanical ladder, coupled with the same prints all around the fire truck told a different story.

We continued on, —into the wasteland of the Texas plains, climbing barbed wire fences and negotiating heavy spring vegetation. We could be traveling for days, if not weeks before we potentially find anything worth holding up in.

2312 hrs

We are taking refuge inside a chain link razor wire fence area for the night. We found it out of blind luck after fighting through cactus and heavy foliage for hours. The sign bolted to the outside of the fence stated the following:

Warning:
Controlled Area, US Government Property
It is unlawful to enter this area without the permission of the installation commander. While on this installation, all personnel and the property under their control are subject to search. This area is patrolled by military working dog teams.

It was approaching nightfall when John ran into it. We had to take turns carrying Laura for the latter part of the day because her little legs were getting tired and she just couldn't keep up. The fenced area couldn't have been more than fifty feet by fifty feet. I hadn't the slightest idea what the government would want with this small area of land, or why such a big deal would be made for it.

I could see the panoramic view of the whole area and saw no sign of life or death besides our group. No building could be seen inside the fence as it was a flat grassy area similar to a regular yard. The crab grass had grown rather high and I suppose if someone were lying down, I would not be able to see them. We had no choice other than sleeping in a tree, and I wasn't much for that option. I grabbed the blankets out of the pack that Tara was carrying and folded them to a width of about three feet wide. I left the length the same.

The fence was around eight feet tall, so it took a couple tries, but I finally got the blankets over the razor wire, so that I could climb over without cutting myself to shreds. As I hit the ground, I pulled my weapon up to the ready and began checking the grass for any danger.

I walked around the inside of the fence, then toward the middle of the area. There was a large manhole type cover just sitting there on the ground. I bent down on one knee and noticed that there was no exterior handle, and if there were, I would definitely not be able to lift it, as there was four inches of steel showing above ground. There were very large hinges present on one side of this odd looking lid. I'm guessing that this lid/cover weighs more than all of us combined. I hear nothing but the sound of nature. The stars are very bright tonight, and the fence is secure. If it doesn't rain, it will be a nice night to sleep under the stars.

March 30th

1517 hrs

Our luck has changed. I woke up this morning to the sound of howling dogs in the distance. No way of knowing if they are wild or domesticated. Made me think of the sign we read on the fence yesterday. I was very curious why a thick steel manhole lid would be sitting inside a razor wire fence in the middle of nowhere, Texas. I told John that I wanted to take a look around outside the fence as on one side it seemed to be clear of trees and shrubs.

Once again, using the blanket technique, I climbed over the fence, with a fully recovered John in tow. John left the .22 with William and the girls and he took the shotgun, because the shotgun wouldn't be a good idea to use through the fence.

The fenced area we came from was about ten feet lower than the hill we were climbing to the clearing. As we topped the small hill, an expansive view unfolded in front of us. There was enough flat land here to land and take off with a small plane, and a fence, similar to the other was about three hundred meters ahead.

As we neared this second fenced in area, we noticed that it was much larger than the one we had spent the night in, and it harbored a small, shed sized brick building with a grey painted steel door and a series of antennas on the roof. When we made it to the fence, John and I noticed a helicopter-landing pad inside the perimeter. Also there was a large patch of blackened grass surrounding what looked like a very large square hole in the ground.

No sign of movement anywhere. We had a clear range of view in all directions. We could even barely make out the tops of the razor wire fence where William and the others were waiting. This was definitely not a base, but it was something. John and I went back for the blankets so that we could scale this new fence. We told William of our discovery and returned to the new area.

Before scaling the fence, I checked the gate just in case. It was locked solid with some sort of cipher locking device. The other area had a large chain and cut resistant padlock on it. I had a feeling that this area was a little more important than the other. We jumped the fence and began checking the perimeter. I walked toward the helicopter pad, keeping my eyes open for any sort of movement. The hole in the ground peaked my curiosity further so John and I decided to check it out. As we edged toward the chasm, I started realizing what this place was.

I had never seen one in real life, but this area might as well have a "Minuteman III" sign posted on the fence. I was standing where a strategic missile had recently launched. The ground was blackened around the gaping horizontal launch doors. I grabbed my flashlight from my pack and checked around the rim of the opening for some sort of access ladder. There was one about three feet below the lip of the thick steel doors that were retracted back sideways into the ground. John held my arm as I hung my leg over into the darkness of the vertical launch shaft. My weapon was slung over my shoulder as I started my descent down into the darkness.

The shaft seemed at least sixty feet deep as it took forever to descend. When I looked up, John seemed a million miles away. I didn't know if I was going crazy at the time, but I could swear I could hear the faint sound of music. I stood at the bottom of the shaft. Shining my light around, I could see dead squirrels that had fallen down the shaft and died from lack of food and water. Dirt and leaves also lined the floor. These doors have been open for a while. Some of the dead squirrels were all but rotted to the bone. I checked the bottom level of the shaft. I noticed an oval shaped door with a wheel in the center on the opposite end from where I was standing. I asked John if he could get down without my help, he didn't answer, but I could see his leg catch the first rung of the ladder as he began his climb down.

As John was on his way down, I grabbed the wheel and moved it counter clockwise (lefty loosy) to see if it would budge. To my surprise, it did. I suppose the three feet thick blast doors at the top of the shaft were good enough to keep intruders out, so they didn't bother locking the insignificant four inch thick oval hatch at the bottom, but why didn't they close the blast doors after launch?

John was now down with me. He stood behind me as I finished turning the wheel crank to unlock the access hatch. I turned it all the way left, and heard the sound of a metal clank as the bolts simultaneously released from the frame. I pulled the door outward and the hiss of air rushed in or out, I could not tell. I opened the door fully, bright light and the sound of music blasted out at John and I.

"It's the end of the world as we know it!" -REM

I guess the end of the world breeds cynicism. Pulling my weapon up to my chest, John and I made our way into the interior of this modern day castle. I had no idea of the layout of the place. I took the lead as we headed toward the source of the music.

All the interior lights were on and we were walking slowly. The song ended...then it began playing again. It was in a constant loop. I had hoped different, because the music gave me a false sense of life. For all I knew the song could have been looping for months, now that I had heard it loop once.

We were closer to the music. It was blaring...

"Wire in a fire, represent the seven games in a government for hire and a combat site..."

Rounding the corner to where we thought the music was coming from; we came to an open door that I estimated to be a foot thick. It looked like a bank vault door. The music was coming from inside that room.

I could see computer panel lights flashing intermittently inside, and the smell of rot was pungent in the air. I gave John the look and I stepped in. Captain Baker was the first corpse to meet my gaze. Tied up in a steel chair, was an Air Force captain with the nametag "Baker" pinned above his right pocket.

He writhed and struggled with the bonds that held him firm. His skin was being torn off in places by the ropes. Another officer lay slumped over a command console with a Berretta 9mm in one hand and half his head missing.

I can only theorize to what happened. Baker had three gunshot wounds to the chest and a cracked skull. As the creature sat there writhing, I grabbed the sidearm out of the other officer's stiff rotting hand. Checking the magazine, I counted eleven rounds. Three for Baker and one for the no name tag "Major Tom" added to fifteen. I suppose Baker was infected, "Major Tom" tied him up, launched the missile, then shot Baker three times in the chest before taking his own life. Of course, it is all speculation and doesn't really matter at this point.

2326 hrs

John and I led the others to the silo, terminated Baker, and took him, along with "Major Tom" to an empty room for temporary storage. Power, food, shelter and water seem to be in abundance.

I have no way of knowing if the Internet backbone is still operational. I am currently utilizing this compound's computer system. Most of the secure consoles are still logged in, and many of the non-secure desktop computers are working. Need to figure out a way to get those blast doors shut. Will be looking for the "keys to the kingdom" in the following days.

Hotel 23

April 1st
0912 hrs

I searched the Baker and "Major Tom" corpses and found numerous personal items and a notepad. Of particular interest was Bakers notepad containing numerous passwords for the different systems in the facility, and a proximity card for entering certain doors.

This facility is powered by the local power grid along with four huge diesel generators. The local power has not gone out in this area. I have located some technical manuals in the desk drawers of the control room. They outline different emergency procedures and capacities for this facility. One of the manuals stated that if this facility is properly stocked, it would provide air, food, water, and shelter for one hundred people for 180 days.

One problem remains; figuring out how everything works, and where everything is. We have not explored the entire facility for fear that there may be more of the undead lurking in the catacombs of the outer reaching compartments. One thing worthy of mention is that all the manuals have the words, "Hotel 23" printed on the covers. A ceremonial wood plaque hangs over the main control console with the same words carved into it in English, and below that in Russian.

The facility galley has a large pantry full of canned food, and numerous items called "C" rations. I have never eaten one, but I have heard about them from some of the old timers I served with before all of this happened. There are also numerous cases of MREs lining the shelves in the back of the walk in pantry.

John, while working with the computer control system, figured out how to operate the remote cameras outside the facility. No luck on finding out how to shut the blast door. Found the main entrance and exit with John's security camera. Unfortunately, it is a quarter of a mile away down the access tunnel, and up an elevator. Worse still, the fact that a hundred undead can be seen on the closed circuit television milling about outside the doors.

April 2nd

2007 hrs

I have located a hand written schematic of the facility today. Some of the rooms don't match the schematic. I assume because some areas may have been added to the facility since it was drawn.

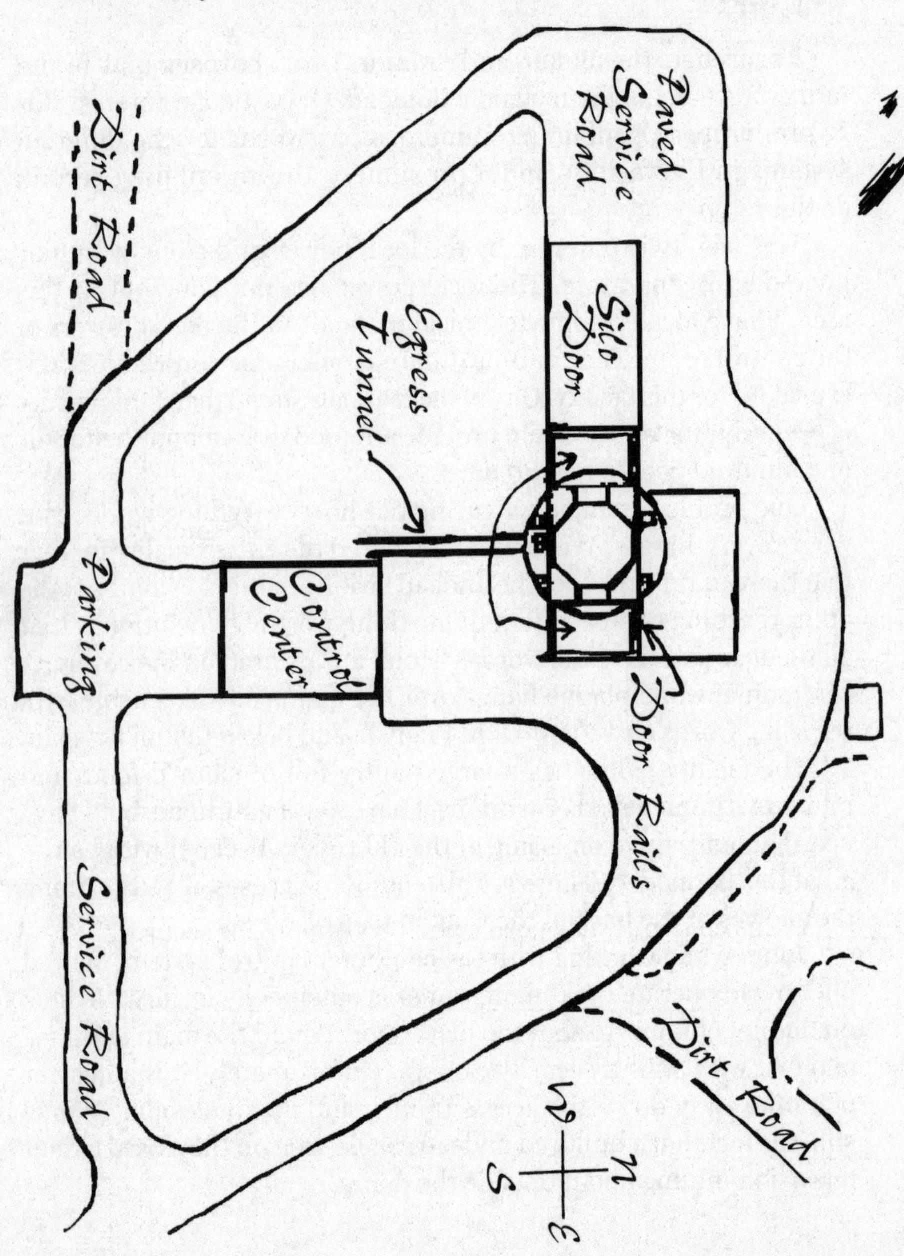

We plan to fully clear out the interior of the bunker by tomorrow. It stinks like rotten flesh and old fruit.

April 4th
1535 hrs

While rummaging through the living area of the silo yesterday, I found Capt. Baker's personal diary. It dates back two years to March. It pretty much outlines everything that happened here since the beginning. I have not read it in its entirety, however I plan to do so in the coming days.

Found this interesting:

Captain Baker, USAF January 10th

"I have been ordered to alert status here at 'Hotel 23.' We keep receiving startling communiqué from missile command regarding our new coordinates for the alternate target packages. Although the coordinates are not in plain language, I have seen enough of them to know that the data we are inputting will not point the nukes overseas. We are confined to the silo on alert status until further notice. Luckily, I thought to bring almost a dozen books with me this time, unlike the last drill we were running. My superiors seem to feel that this epidemic may pose a real problem to our security.

We made an attempt to thoroughly clean the interior today. From time to time, I can hear a mechanical/electrical sound kick in from another area inside the bunker. I have a feeling it is some sort of air filtration system. We cleared most of the silo yesterday, all except the room marked, "environmental control." There is a heavy steel door with a cipher lock blocking access to the interior. The notepad taken from the officer a couple days ago had no useful codes for this particular door. John found a folder on the desktop of one of the launch control computers.

The non-classified computers are using Windows, however the secure tempest resistant boxes are running some form of Linux that I have never seen. John has been using some sort of DOS like non-GUI (graphical user interface) to explore the computer. He has been able to bring up numerous color aerial photographs of the same area (unknown), only it seems like every time, he accesses the folder with the photographs, and selects the same filename, it shows a slightly different photo, i.e. different cloud placement, or some other minute detail.

Also on the list to access is a large seven-foot tall, thick steel safe marked ARMORY. Unfortunately there is a rather large padlock in place on the front of the safe, temporarily barring access. I haven't really gotten a chance to get to know Tara, but she did reveal just how curious of a person she really is. She did not like the idea of not being able to see what was in the safe, and searched the bunker for three hours, digging through boxes trying to find something that would be useful in cutting the lock. No joy.

On a side note, all of the toilets in this facility are similar to airplane latrines. Dry bowls. I suppose it conserves water. Which reminds me of the water supply here. We found a large rectangular tank in the diesel generator rooms marked "potable water." Using the butt of my rifle, I tapped the side of it until a hollow sound resonated through the chamber. It was over 3/4ths of the way full. The tank is roughly 20ft x 10ft x 5ft. I will do calculations in the coming days as to how much water we can and should be using.

A Picture is Worth a Thousand Words

April 6th
2144 hrs

It should have been obvious the reason the photos that John was pulling up on the secure UNIX computer were changing. They were near real time satellite imagery. John figured out what it was last night and also figured out how to zoom the photos down to what the computer indicates is .2-meter resolution. Using rough coordinates in the road atlas, we were able to see detailed photography of what was left of the San Antonio area.

It was difficult at first to interpret the overhead angle of the photos. Also, the color wasn't tweaked very well, making the photos look a little off. After numerous command line inputs, John zoomed down to a one thousand meter resolution and we were able to see a good section of what was left of downtown. The photo was a few minutes old according to the time stamp, due to the fact that the satellite was configured to automatically photograph a certain footprint at a certain time. John couldn't figure out how to get the bird to take a snapshot on demand.

Studying the photo, I could make out numerous destroyed buildings, and even some of those creatures that must have wandered back after the initial blast, attracted by the sound and light. I could also make out a group of them huddled around something. John zoomed in the best he could to the center of the group of corpses.

The group was fighting over the carcass of a large rat. I suppose a picture really is worth a thousand words. John and I plan to go city by city, entering coordinates and attempting to gather any information we can on what cities were destroyed and which ones still stand. This will take some time, but worth the peace of mind, or lack thereof.

Jan and William have settled into one of the larger compartments, with Laura. John told them it would be fine by him if Annabelle slept with Laura at night. John knew the dog helped Laura deal with our situation, as Annabelle was something familiar from a world long fucked.

Yesterday, Tara and I went topside to check the perimeter, as the camera near where we climbed in only covered the launch bay doors. Kind of ironic how John can figure out how to look at a dead man's wristwatch from a thousand miles away with a satellite, but can't seem to figure out how to get our back door closed. I have to give him credit as he has proven himself a good friend and a very adaptable person.

April 8th
2324 hrs

After a few days of figuring out coordinates with many failed attempts, we have come across cities on the satellite photos that are confirmed destroyed by either nukes, or more conventional MOABs.

I wanted to use the birds to see my home back in Arkansas, but they didn't seem to work above a certain longitude. San Antonio, New Orleans, San Diego, Los Angeles, Dallas, and Orlando and probably New York have been destroyed and we have confirmed that dead walk the ruined streets. This is a definite blow to the group's morale, including my own. John and I, using a larger resolution in order to see a more wide view of the cities, saw mass devastation. Not even one of the photos displayed any living human. Some of the groups we were seeing reminded me of old photos of the Woodstock crowds. There was no way to count, but I estimate there are millions of undead in highly radiated areas of ruined cities. There is no telling how many walk in unaffected areas of the United States. We are hopelessly outnumbered and worse, there seems to be no fragment of any government remaining.

John and I attempted to gather satellite intelligence on the more northern states, but were unsuccessful due to the fact of the limitations of the satellite footprint (area of effective satellite view). However, I was able to find some information on the fate of New York City.

Upon closer inspection of the command and control area, I found a black briefcase with a double spin lock set to the numbers 205 on both sides wedged between two consoles. The case was unlocked, and inside was a printed message.

I suppose the government used the space and missile command to take up the slack for the "rogue" pilots. They must have foreseen this coming as Baker commented on his new target packages well before the pilots decided to disobey orders.

TOP SECRET

RTTUZYUW RUHPNQN0765 0312376Z TTTTTT-ZZZZ
DE NNNOASA 155
Z 311700Z JAN
FM DEPT OF AF SPC MSL CMD
TO ALSIOP ESI LONE STAR
INFO ZEN/NORTH AMERICAN AIR DEFENSE//AFSC-OPE-MA//
ZEN/HQ LACKLAND AFB TX//GCGS/MARS//
BT
T O P S E C R E T //N02763//
SUBJ: COMMAND LAUNCH AUTHORITY //MAGENTA ROCKET//
A. EX. ORDER 23765 WASHINGTON DC 311600Z
JAN (CMB 16-98)
B. NTP 8(C), ART. 830, SAMPLE MESSAGE 3.

1. AUTHORITY FOR DOMESTIC RELEASE OF TACTICAL
NUCLEAR WEAPONS HAS BEEN AUTHORIZED BY THE
PRESIDENT OF THE UNITED STATES.
AUTHENTICATION CODING TO FOLLOW
FLASH TRANSMISSION.

2. TARGET PACKAGE BISCT. 870E57E86YF CONFIRMED.
P.L.
LOCATION: NEW YORK CITY, NEW YORK.

3. ORIGINAL TACTICAL WEAPONS SCHEDULED FOR NYC
WERE BROKEN ARROW. PILOTS ROGUE.

BT

April 11th

1233 hrs

Still no key to the small arms locker. I am debating on whether or not it is worth it to go out into an urban area to retrieve the necessary equipment needed to cut the lock off. A cutting torch would be optimal, but I doubt I would be able to procure one. It may have to be a hacksaw. Bolt cutters would be useless, as the lock bolt is so large, no cutters I have seen would get through it.

John found the access code needed to get into the environmental compartment. It was embedded in the file system in the facility control folders. As with any new area we were very cautious about going in. John held the door and waited for me to give the signal. I dreaded shooting anything in this compartment, as I did not want the ricochet to damage any vital systems inside. John slung the door open, it was very dark.

I pulled my NVGs down over my eyes, and switched them on. Walking in, I saw no danger. The room was very clean. Finding the light switch on the wall, I pulled the goggles back up above my eyes and flipped the switch. It took a few seconds for the fluorescent bulbs to kick in. The room touted a huge air cleansing system, of which I have no idea how to adjust or maintain. There were equipment racks holding all sorts of environmental monitoring gadgets. Right of the bat, I noticed two different varieties of gas masks, and also five Geiger counter devices sitting side by side in a neat row. The gas masks were without filters, as the filters were still sealed in the tins sitting next to the masks. I counted ten gas masks of both types, twenty in all.

On the floor there were several boxes that had "C.B.R. suit" stamped on the side. Using my knife, I carefully cut away the tape and found that each box contained ten olive drab chemical, biological, and radiological protective suits, sealed in plastic. Also in the box, was a set of specifications and instructions on how long and how much exposure a human can expect to take while wearing the suits.

It is clear that this facility was designed to endure a nuclear attack. I just don't understand why there were only two officers stationed here, and no other VIP survivors. Maybe the world fell apart to quickly, or this outpost wasn't even on the map. That brings up another important item. It was only yesterday when I found out where we were. It seemed like a long time ago when we left the Bahama Mama, and blindly ran into this place after what seemed like days of walking, taking turns carrying Laura and Annabelle. Using satellite imagery, John found our location. We estimated our general direction of travel from the shoreline, and used the atlas to enter in coordinates.

We first had to find the boat. We then adjusted our coordinates and resolution northwest in baby steps until we found the wreckage site where the fireman was hanging from the hydraulic ladder. After this, we kept walking the coordinates, painstakingly northwest again, until we came upon the facility.

It was easily seen, as the gaping hole of the launch bay was an obvious flag. John marked the exact coordinates on a piece of paper. Just to make sure we were looking at the right photo, I took a roll of toilet paper up topside, made sure the area was clear, and made a giant letter "X" with the toilet paper near the open launch bay doors.

After about fifteen minutes of waiting, John re-entered the coordinates and sure enough, the toilet paper "X" was immediately visible from the one hundred meter resolution we had entered. Keeping the same coordinates, we zoomed out to two hundred kilometers of resolution. Though we could not see our facility, we knew it was center screen, because that is how the program works.

We were able to determine using the atlas, and the photo, that we were near the small town of Nada, TX. The bad news was that we were also about sixty miles southwest of Houston. Houston was not destroyed in the nuclear campaign and remembering the photos we pulled up on the 8th, we knew it was crawling with the undead. Using the CCT cameras we can monitor undead movement at the main entrance, however using the satellite photos, we can attempt to monitor the big picture now that we have our exact coordinates.

"Knock, Knock"

April 12th
2219 hrs

I have not mentioned/documented much about the entertainment value of the facility. There is a lounge area, equipped with television, VCR and DVD player. Numerous DVDs line the inside of the wood case the TV is sitting on. After opening the case and checking the contents, I came across one of my old favorites, Omega Man on VHS. For some reason, I just cannot bring myself to watch it, sort of like watching a war movie while still on the battlefield.

I have taken to running the perimeter fence during the day. I check the CCT monitor prior to going outside, to make sure the crowd is still where I saw them last, hopelessly clawing at the thick steel door at the front of the facility. After almost fifty laps around the perimeter fence, I come in, and take a very short shower. I usually time myself so that I can conserve water. This reminds me of boot camp, and officer candidate school, where I had to put the shampoo in my hair before getting in the shower to save time in the shower. I have my time down to one minute.

The others don't seem to have the discipline, or the concept of conservation. I can't expect everyone to act like a machine I suppose. Perhaps that is my problem lately. I have been so shell-shocked that I have reverted to logic and emotionless response to deal with the situation at hand.

After checking the facility thoroughly a few days ago, we now have a suitable entrance to get in and out without having to climb the silo ladder every time. There were stairs that led up to where we thought was the shed sized brick building with a grey painted steel door. Since this access door led to the surface near the launch bay doors, we thought it best and safer to use it.

Tara and I spent time together today. We are becoming friends. Under close supervision, She and I let Annabelle and Laura outside to play in the perimeter area. Yesterday afternoon John and I went outside. Using some twine and four wooden stakes taken from the maintenance compartment, we made a make shift fence around the launch bay door area. I didn't want any of us accidentally falling in. Obviously, we still have not figured out the coding needed to operate the bay doors. John seems to know how to access the right area of the computer system, but he just doesn't want to make a mistake and open the main doors in front of the complex. Opening Pandora's Box would let hundreds of those demons inside, forcing us to quarantine a large part of the compound.

After watching Laura play outside with Annabelle, I forgot about the undead for a while. It wasn't until half an hour later, when the wind brought the moans of the dead to my attention did I remember the dire circumstances that brought is here to Hotel 23. I rushed them back into the facility just as the wind started carrying the smell of rot along with the symphony of horrible moans.

April 14th

2357 hrs

We experienced a blackout here for approximately two hours. The battery backups kicked in, providing some red battle lighting inside the complex. I suppose the power grid may finally be failing in this area. No way to determine. Power came back on at 2330. I am sure the system is automated, as I doubt any faithful electrical plant worker would be manning his/her post in times like these.

April 15th

1920 hrs

I am going out tonight to recon the area with NVGs. I will be avoiding the high undead population area of the front blast door. That area is a quarter of a mile away over a small hill. John will be watching with the remote cameras.

I told him that if there is any sign of trouble, I would lead them away from the complex and not to worry. It is not like they can see in the dark anyway. Perhaps I am becoming complacent, and I am underestimating them. I know that in large numbers they are lethal. On that matter, they are lethal in numbers of one.

Today I heard the strange mechanical sound four times. On one occasion I rushed to the environmental control room to see if that was the source. It wasn't. The sound is coming from somewhere in the bowels of this complex. It may be some sort of pump, or backup system, I cannot be sure. This is the first year I have ever been late on my taxes.

April 16th
1409 hrs

I patrolled the area last night. Before going out, I checked out the satellite photos in detail from the day before with John. The area is surrounded by two fences, and the main entrance is only accessible through an underground tunnel, or by walking up to it from outside the second fence. I also noticed that on the photos, there appeared to be a small group of bodies on the ground at the northeast side of the complex. I went up the stairs to the exterior access. I asked John to shut off the lights in my area to allow them to adjust to the dark before I went out. I waited twenty minutes for full night vision adjustment.

I slipped on the NVGs, tightened the straps and opened up the hatch. The cool night air smelled of spring honeysuckles. I stepped through the threshold into their world. After dogging the hatch behind me, I took the blanket from my shoulder and flung it over the fence in the same spot we originally climbed over.

I had the codes to the gate, but I didn't want to have to work the cipher lock during an adrenaline rush. The blanket was a safer means of traversing the fence in this situation. By now, the blanket had been cut up in many places and wouldn't be good for anything but a fire after a couple more uses. I left it slung over the razor wire as my boots hit the ground and I started walking counter clockwise around the perimeter.

I could see the eyes of numerous nocturnal animals in the area when I switched on the infrared on the NVGs. Rabbits and mice, and squirrels were thick in this area at night. This is something to keep in mind for future food possibilities. I rounded the first corner to the fence, and walked.

As I left the area I was familiar with, I stepped into part of the complex I had seen. There was a three hundred yard gap between our fence and the other fence I had never been to. Right where I stood, I estimated that John was eighty feet below. I could see the bright lights of the security cameras at the corner of our fence as they followed me. They also used infrared, so they were like beacons to my goggles. I approached fence number two after almost a minute of jogging. I edged up toward the northeast corner. The moans and the smell of the dead strengthened as I approached. I was now out of range of most of the facility cameras, sans the main access door.

I could now see the bodies piled up outside fence number two, and faintly in the distance I could also see the main mass of the dead relentlessly pounding on the main access door. I crouched down, and quietly approached the corpses. The nearer I got, the more it made sense. The fence had numerous breaks in it from what I assume was automatic weapons fire aimed from the inside out. The corpses on the ground fell victim to someone inside the fence firing through at them. The bodies on the ground had been there for a long time. Maggots and other insects covered their bare skin.

I scanned the interior of fence number two for the gunman that was responsible. I could see nothing inside the fence but tall grass. This fence must enclose something important, but I could not see any large steel hatches similar to the first fence we found. I can't help thinking that whoever shot these ghouls retreated back into the darkness of the bunker for safety. We have explored the facility and found nothing else inside it, living or dead. My mind wondered to the intermittent mechanical sound.

I checked the fence where the damage was present, and found that though it was damaged; nothing bigger than a human arm could fit through it. There were dried blood stains and chunks of skin on the jagged edges of the damaged wire, indicating that some of them were in fact putting their arms through it, attempting to reach their executioner.

Quietly, I turned around and made my way back the way I came. Instead of going straight to fence number one, I crossed over between the two fences, taking a different route. I came out between the fences on the west side of the complex. Again I took notice of the long, level grassy strip. I noticed it when we first found this area. I could easily take off or land a small aircraft here. It wouldn't be a bad idea to try and find one just in case. After all, flying is not like riding a bike, it is a perishable skill. I jumped the fence, retrieved the blanket, entered the complex and commenced to tell the others what I saw.

April 19th

1211 hrs

I returned last night from a three-day trip to scavenge for supplies and needed equipment. I am injured and once again, nearly did not survive this outing. John faired somewhat better than I with only a scratched face. One of them, in all its flailing, scraped him. We were on foot most of the time.

Using the atlas and the air navigation chart I had from before, we were able to determine the location to the nearest airfield. According to our chart, a small private airstrip called Eagle Lake existed 20 miles NNE from Hotel 23. The night prior to our departure, John and I were able to pull up a satellite photo of the general area, and sure enough, two parallel concrete runways could be seen on the satellite visuals. A hangar and what appeared to be two small aircraft were parked near the small tower. As we zoomed out, the faint thread of I-10 could also be seen roughly eight miles north of the airfield. We knew transportation might be necessary to return safely, so we zoomed in on the strip of I-10 directly north of the airfield. Cars were haphazardly stopped all over the interstate. This was the main vein that ran between the ruins of San Antonio, and the city of Houston.

There were droves of undead on the interstate. John and I thought it highly unlikely that going to the interstate would be fruitful in any way. The cool morning air of April rushed into the hatch as we turned the locking crank. The flowers were blooming, and it looked like a beautiful day. John and I were loaded down with equipment. He entered the cipher lock code that unlocked the gate, linking us once again to a world where we were not welcome.

Sticking to the grassy and wooded areas, we made our way. As we neared the main entrance for the first time, we were able to see our door greeters in person, without the help of digital enhancement. John and I took turns with the binoculars as we watched from the distant bushes. Two words could probably sum them up; hungry, angry. I doubt anyone could fathom where their undying grudge toward the living originated. I didn't care to know either way.

I was repulsed as they clawed and pounded on the heavy steel blast doors, breaking fingernails and leaving a brown liquid behind with each scratch and thud. Some of them were clearly agitated and were shoving others out of the way so they too could get a chance at turning their arms into stumps.

Another startling fact worthy of mention was that one of them was using a rock as a bludgeon on the steel door. The rock was the size of a baseball, and the creature steadily and unrelentingly pounded away. I knew why we had never heard it before. The exterior blast door was just one of three doors that separated the outside world from our group inside Hotel 23. These creatures clearly retain some sort of primal sense about them.

John and I continued our northerly track toward Eagle Lake. Prior to leaving Hotel 23, we attempted to print out the satellite photo to bring with us as a visual reference. For some reason the security feature inside the control console would not allow printing operations that accessed the image intelligence (IMINT) folders. We were forced to draw notes and sketches on our existing atlas depicting landmarks of interest.

After contemplating the bludgeoning corpse for a few minutes, we continued our journey northward toward Eagle Lake. The terrain was rough and unforgiving as we dredged our way through, intermittently cutting our legs on nature's barbed wire. After an hour of hiking, careful to remain just out of sight of the two-lane road, we came upon a group of crosses erected in the center of a field. There were four crosses of varying height. There were three undead corpses bound to the crosses, as the fourth was dead. It appeared that the local avian life had picked a majority of this corpse's brain right out of its head.

Eerily, the other three corpses locked onto us simultaneously as we approached. Their snarling heads swiveled laboriously as they struggled to hold them up and follow our movements. One of them was not restrained as well as the other two and its legs flailed wildly in an attempt to free itself from the prison of crossed timber and restraints. John and I knew that if we shot them, it would without a doubt bring more to our position. The crosses swayed in their makeshift holes as the dead struggled for freedom.

We decided to leave the area and continue north. As we left this cursed field, I wondered what treacherous group of miscreants bothered to take the time and make the crosses, post them, and then crucify four dead on the cross. My mind then stumbled upon a very disturbing thought: What if they weren't dead when they were crucified?

I didn't reveal this to John, as there was no point at us both being terrified of nothing. As we approached the boundaries of the field, we climbed the barbwire fence, and headed out into the open plains of Texas.

I don't know if it was the prospect of flying again that forced me out here among them, or if it was just the need to see what was happening. I knew what was going on well enough. We were fucked, and there was nothing that could be said or done about it. Even a large spider is no match for an army of ants.

We headed toward the hangar for the simple reason that we needed some specific supplies, i.e. hacksaw for the weapons locker, and because, having an aircraft at Hotel 23 would be a very good escape vehicle. Another reason was that if we managed to clear out the undead in front of the blast doors, it would also be a good means by which to scout.

I thought back to the satellite photos of the airfield. Of course, they were taken from a straight down angle due to the fact that the camera was in space. I was decent at recognizing aircraft silhouettes, however, just being able to see the top view wing profile, I was not sure if I was looking at two Cessna 172s, or 152s. It didn't matter. The thought of being able to fly again gave me a positive feeling. John and I continued our journey to Eagle Lake airfield. It was 1900 hrs when we first smelled the aroma. It wasn't the rotting dead smell. It was the familiar smell of lake water being brought from the northern afternoon breeze. As we topped the next hill, a great watery expanse appeared before us.

According to the atlas, Eagle Lake was not a very big body of water. It seemed to welcome us, although after my experience on the docks, god only knew what was lurking in its dark depths. We were near the airfield, but John and I knew we needed to find a place to sleep before it got dark. There was a road on the other side of the lake. I took out my binoculars, and saw that a large steel greyhound bus was pulled over on the side of the road along with several other smaller cars.

I studied the bus for several minutes, making damn sure there was no movement, in or around it. I handed the binoculars to John and he did the same. We carefully edged our way around the shorter side of the lake that led to the road. The sun was getting dangerously low as we neared the two-lane highway. There were numerous cars strewn about, but no undead movement. I knew they were out there, I just couldn't see them. John and I held our weapons ready as we edged toward the Greyhound. No chances. I knelt down on my knee, weapon pointed outward and whispered to John to stand on my shoulder and look inside the bus to make sure.

After repeating this in six foot intervals all the way to the back of the bus, we were satisfied it was empty. We were edgy. I wasn't particularly looking forward to seeing another one of these rotting fuckers, but I knew it was going to happen sometime on this trip. I walked over to the door of the bus, and easily pulled it open. The locking bar wasn't set at the driver's seat, and the keys were still in it. I highly doubt that the battery still worked, but I didn't care, this was just our hotel for the night.

I stepped onto the bus, still careful. John followed. We shut the heavy steel/glass door, and pushed the locking bar in, making it impossible to open the door from the outside. The hair stood up on the back of my neck as my eyes caught a glimpse of something in the aisle on the back row. A human arm was lying across the walkway. It appeared in the advanced stages of decomposition.

John stayed back, making sure to keep an eye on the perimeter of the bus as I checked it out. Weapon trained, I approached the rear of the bus. At two-thirds the length of the bus, I saw that the arm was just that, only an arm. I put on my nomex gloves, and quietly opened a window and tossed the fleshy bony piece of shit out. It appeared that someone had wiped their ass all over the back seat, but it was only dried brown blood. I gave John the thumbs up and we proceeded to quietly set up camp in here (after I checked under every single seat twice).

I had two sets of AA batteries for the NVGs, but I was rationing them, and only using NVGs when absolutely necessary, so that night was spent in darkness sans the moonlight. John and I whispered to each other, talking most of the night about how we were going to handle the next day. The airfield was not marked on the road atlas. We were going to have to extrapolate the location of the airfield by the air navigation chart that I still had. The atlas and the air chart were in two totally different scales, so we knew it could take some time to find it exactly.

That night I went to sleep to the sound of rain on the steel roof. It wasn't until 0300 hrs when I was startled awake by lightening flash and thunder. I wiped my eyes, and regained consciousness as I peered out the semi-tinted windows of the bus. The lightening was becoming frequent, and I was glad that we were inside. Then another flash, and I could see the outline of a human roughly 20 meters away. This was one of those necessary times, so I quickly donned the NVGs. It wasn't a human; it was the lone corpse of a drifter that still wore a pack on his back. I could see his cheekbones jutting through his leathery skin as the thing shifted its weight back and forth. The backpack seemed to be of the type that not only fastened over the shoulders, but also with a chest strap to keep it steady while he walked. The creature's teeth were showing in an eternal grin as the water dripped from its lifeless body.

It couldn't see us. John was still asleep. I didn't bother to disturb him. It wasn't long before the drifter moved on, into the darkness of the Texas night to the next stop.

The next morning (17th), we quietly packed our things and started to head out. On the way out the door, I asked John to cover me as I tried to turn over the bus engine out of sheer curiosity. True it would make noise, but I just wanted to know if the battery still worked after all these months. I turned the key and held the starter switch. The bus made not one sound. It was dead like last night's drifter. John and I left the scene in search of the airfield.

After a couple of hours of searching, we found the runways. It wasn't that far off the main road. It looked exactly like the satellite photographs portrayed it, so I was nearly certain we had the right field. In the distance, I could make out the shape of two aircraft parked near the tower. Cautiously, we approached the airfield perimeter fence, making sure to stop and listen at regular intervals. This fence was not topped with razor wire. John and I easily climbed it and set foot inside. We could see for hundreds of yards. There was no movement anywhere. We felt confident about our safety for the time being.

This area seemed to be nearly devoid of all undead activity. I knew that I-10 was a few miles north of our position and the satellite photos indicated a large undead population there. Perhaps they drew each other to I-10 in a similar way that water drops seem to attract one another. It might have been the noise they were all making. It could have been my imagination, but every now and then I thought I could hear the wind carry their familiar macabre sound from far into the distance.

My main concern were the two aircraft, and if they were flyable. We edged closer and closer to the tower, eyes trained on the two birds, both parked close together. One of them was definitely a 172. The other was a 152, the slightly less powerful Cessna. I was no expert on how to repair them, but they seemed to look in decent shape from where we stood. Once again, I pulled out the binoculars to examine the perimeter from our vantage point. The hangars were closed and I heard no commotion from that direction. The tower's tinted windows were very intimidating, as I could not tell whether or not one of those things was frothing at the mouth at us from up there. It had to be done though, as we knew we were going to spend the night of the 17th inside the tower for protection.

Once again, John and I stepped up to the tower doors. John covered me as I carefully turned the steel handle opening the door. It was dark inside. I switched on the flashlight on my weapon and began clearing the stairwell. No sign of blood, no sign of struggle. The tower was abandoned.

As we neared the top of the tower, the feeling of dread soon left us. It was empty. Being inside the control tower brought back memories of our escape. That seemed like years ago. There was no power inside the tower, although I could see that an exterior light was on at the hangar. Must have been a tripped breaker. I never bothered to find out.

Our next order of business was to check the hangars, as more than likely the tools and materials we were after were inside. It was approaching 1400 hrs, and it was exceptionally hot that day. With complacency set in heavy, John and I lackadaisically approached the first hangar. I signaled John to cover me and I slung the door open. It was then our lazy attitude almost killed us.

A rotted corpse in a white apron and undershirt came barreling out of the doorway with hedge trimming shears clamped in its left hand. It had no idea it was using them as a weapon as it charged John, seemingly oblivious to my presence. The thing stumbled quickly and fell onto John, gnashing its rotting teeth. The cutting shears cut John's cheek. I could hear the sound of some other movement inside the hangar. I kicked the creature off of John and spun around to the open doorway that was devoid of light. I thought John was fine, but apparently the fall had knocked him

out. The thing that I had kicked off of John now had a new target in mind...me.

Again it charged in a slow stumble toward me. It was too late. By the time I reacted to the familiar gurgling sound it made, it had already inadvertently stabbed me in the ribs with the trimming shears. I spun around in red-hot anger. After kicking the thing in the chest, knocking it to the ground very near John, I trained my sights between the eyes and neutralized it. The brains looked like blue cauliflower right before the dust adhered to the sticky mess. The shears were still in the creature's hand, as I assume they had been for months and now will be forever.

I knelt down near John and slapped him in the face a few times. His blood was all over my hands. Although my wound was worse than his, he seemed to be bleeding more. I checked the shears. They seemed dry, other than our fresh blood. A sound from the reminded me of the other danger we could be facing. I wasn't going to leave John knocked out.

I kept slapping him until he finally woke up. I helped him to his feet and told him to keep a look out. The light I had seen previously on the hangar was above the open door. Two large hangar doors were on both sides of the open doorway. I planned to enter the hangar and hit the door switch, bathing the inside with sunlight.

As I entered the doorway, I caught a glimpse of one of them. I had no choice but to take it out. My muzzle flash revealed more of them. The flash was bright and it temporarily burned the image of six other corpses into the back of my retina. I reached over for the switch and hit it. No joy. I tried the one below it and heard the rumble of the "garage door" sound.

I made for the door with my back to John, pointing the weapon ahead of me into the dying darkness of the hangar. Looking over my shoulder I could see that John was very light headed and leaning on his rifle. I yelled at him to get back with me. It was game time. I readied my rifle and waited for them to come. The first one made the roll call. I killed her with one shot. More soon followed, excited by their first sight of food in months. With outstretched arms, they gave chase. John was trying to shoot, but missed every shot. I finished most of them in one shot, however two of them I missed twice. The last creature fell four feet from where I stood.

There were eight expired undead at the bay doors and on the dirt in front of the hangar. I had killed them all. I checked my magazine and reloaded. John was regaining his composure, and the bleeding on his cheek had stopped. He nodded to me that he was ok, and that we needed to get these bodies out of sight, because the dead were not the only ones that could have heard those gunshots. We both knew what the other was thinking...the crosses.

We dragged the bodies inside a corner of the hangar, cutting shears and all. After looking around for a few minutes we found a blue tarp to disguise their demonic presence. I forgot about my wound until John stumbled across a first aid kit mounted next to a fire extinguisher.

Using my knife to break the seal, I commenced to taking out what I needed. I took out the iodine, the medical tape and the gauze. I unzipped my flight suit and pulled it to my waist. I could see the dark blood clearly through my dark green undershirt. I was afraid to pull up my shirt...Slowly, I slid the shirt up over my left rib cage, and saw that it wasn't that bad, but it definitely needed first aid. I shook the iodine, opened it and then liberally applied it to the wound. It was cold and stung a little. It didn't need stitches. The iodine turned my skin bright orange. I applied the gauze and tightly wound the tape around my rib cage until I was satisfied.

Checking the fence, John and I noticed that in the distance gathered a group of three undead. They were drawn to the sound of the gunfire. They were too far away to see us, but it was still an uneasy feeling knowing they were there and reacting to our audible presence.

After finding numerous supplies, i.e. hacksaw, wrenches, fuel siphon, spray lubricant and an old leather bomber jacket, we proceeded to look through the publications room of the hangar. Inside we found numerous Cessna checklists, some of them outdated but they would work in this situation. Also of importance was a maintenance manual covering the Cessna 172 and the 152. John and I took our bounty and headed toward the aircraft. Now there were four at the fence. We were at the aircraft and I immediately began to run the aircraft checklist to see if it was even operational.

It took me a few minutes to accomplish, however, after three attempts at engine start, the prop finally turned over and it sputtered to life. I got all the systems running and checked the fuel. I was sitting at half capacity, or two hours of airtime. I calculated that Hotel 23 was only about a twenty-minute flight, so fuel wasn't the issue. The undead quickly growing in numbers outside of the fence was. I shut down the engine and John and I proceeded back to the hangar to get a fuel can so that we could siphon fuel from the 152 to the 172. There were now ten at the fence. They were not trying to get in, but they were milling about, drawn to the noise of gunshots and aircraft engines.

John and I grabbed the can and proceeded to accomplish the tedious task of siphoning twenty-two gallons of fuel to top off the aircraft. After twenty gallons, the 152 was bone dry. Oh well. Doing quick math in my head, I knew we had roughly three hours and forty-five minutes of airtime before she glided out of the sky. We loaded up the back seat of the aircraft with our equipment. We also stuffed ever nook and cranny of the avionics bay with everything we could fit. I also took some oil for the aircraft from the maintenance hangar, as you just never know.

As a final preparation, I took the battery out of the 152, and squeezed it into the pile of supplies in the back seat. We were running heavy, but I had experience with that and this time we had a real runway, not a dirt track. It was getting late. There were only thirteen of them at the fence, so I doubted that they would breach it. As we performed our final preparation on the aircraft, we heard faint automatic weapons fire in the distance. Upon hearing this sound, many of the creatures gave up at the fence and wondered off toward the new sound.

Who was it? John and I had no idea. Worst case, (and it probably was worst case) it was the crazy fuckers that crucified those poor bastards in that field a few miles north of Hotel 23. John and I prepped everything we could and retired to the control tower for a restless night of sleep.

I woke up the next morning to a shooting pain in my ribs. John's face looked much better, but my cut was getting infected. I cleaned it again, and applied clean dressing. It was 1000 hrs that morning before I felt like leaving the tower. There was no sign of undead at the fence now, and John and I did not hear any gunfire the night before. Now came the obvious problem. How the hell were we going to fly the plane back, land at the grass strip next to H23, get out of the aircraft and then climb the fence without getting eaten?

John and I thought on this for a few hours and narrowed down a night approach with night vision goggles as our best option. I expressed my concern that the loud noise of the engine would draw them to our position regardless of night or day. It was then that John asked, "Well, can you land it with the engine off?" I laughed at him, and told him that I didn't know and that I had never tried to land an aircraft with the engine cut except during flight training under controlled situations. I thought on this for a good while before agreeing that it might work.

John and I patiently waited for the night to come. It wasn't until 2050 hrs on the 18th of April, that we decided it was time to go home. That night, as we loaded up our bedrolls and random gear from the tower into the aircraft, we heard gunfire again. This time the weapons fire was closer, much closer. John and I could also hear something that sounded like vehicle engines between the gun bursts. We hopped in, locked our harnesses and I proceeded to get our asses home. I knew that we would easily be able to find H23 because of the security cameras. Using the NVGs I was able to see anything that shined in the infrared wavelength, just like it were a beacon.

We instructed William to make sure the cameras were on and infrared capable before they retired to bed each night. This was our failsafe, our breadcrumb trail that would lead us home. I taxied her to the runway, careful to skip the step that turns the landing lights on. No strobes, no lights, nothing to give away our position.

As I centered her nose wheel on the centerline of the runway, I could see grainy green images of numerous human figures on the other side of the fence. Neither John, nor I wanted to find out if they were friend or foe. I released the breaks, and at fifty knots indicated airspeed, I pulled her nose up and we were once again airborne. Using the air navigation chart, I began to point the nose of the aircraft in the direction of H23.

Just as we cleared the end of the runway, I could see automatic muzzle flash on the ground below. I had no idea if they were shooting at me, or if they were defending themselves. Thinking back to the crosses, I leaned toward the former.

It wasn't long until I could see the glow of the numerous security

cameras in my NVGs. I made one circling pass to get my bearings, and then I climbed to 2,500 feet and began my circling approach. At 2,500 feet, I reluctantly cut my engine, and knew we were going to be on the ground whether we liked it or not. I didn't know how to air start this plane. This was a one-way ticket back to sea level. My right wing was parallel with the western fence (two western corner cameras). I kept checking my altimeter, and airspeed. Eighty knots, 1,500 feet.

I circled again, this time with a steeper angle of bank, because I was too high. I bled off some altitude and came around on final approach at six hundred feet. We were definitely falling faster than I was comfortable with. I could see H23 off my left wing. The NVGs were shit for depth perception, so I had to keep my eye on my altimeter. (I set it to sea level before I took off). Three hundred, two hundred, one hundred, 70 knots...

At ten feet, I flared the aircraft back to soften the landing. The prop was still wind milling as my main gear set down, followed too quickly by my front wheel. We slammed down hard, and loose shit flew everywhere inside the cockpit. I kept her straight as I slowly applied what was left of the hydraulic brakes to slow our speed.

Hydraulics don't work well with the engine off line. I could have cared less about the gear we left behind. All I had with me was my rifle, as I left the plane in the middle of the field and sprinted to the fence with John in tow behind.

We got to the fence and John entered the code. The mechanical clinking sound indicated that the cipher was unlocked. We entered the fence, shut it behind us, and finally, we were safer. I walked through the hatch last night into Tara's open arms and concerned eyes as she gazed at my bloody clothing. I spent most of this morning resting and getting medically tended to by Jan. She seemed to think that stitches were a good idea and abruptly re-opened my wound. She cleaned it up and proceeded to painfully stitch the laceration. I didn't argue. I simply took a few shots of Captain Baker's Captain Morgan to ease the pain.

April 21st

2118 hrs

We spent the day hiding the aircraft with brush and grass, and moving the supplies from the plane to H23. John is vigorously examining satellite photos to try and determine the identity of our ground to air attackers. Tara has stuck close to me since we got back. Tomorrow we will attempt to access the weapons locker with the hacksaw.

April 24th

2041 hrs

All is silent in the hotel. The infection around my rib area is receding. It is itching and feeling hot, vice the familiar soreness of deep infection. Jan tells me that in a week, she will probably be cutting them out for me. To bad for me, she used regular sewing thread. On the morning of the 22nd, William, John and I took turns sawing the huge lock off of the steel weapons locker. I sawed for ten-minutes, the other two did the same.

We applied lubricant to the saw to keep it from burning up and breaking the tips of the saw blade. It took almost an hour to cut the lock. In my mind, I half expected a gaggle of corpses to come falling out of the locker when we opened the door. Of course, this was not the case. We were in luck. Inside this large locker was a cache of military grade small arms. There were five M-16s, and one of them was equipped with an M-203 grenade launcher. Not being a trained infantry soldier, I had some research to do long before I ever try to deploy the grenade launcher function.

Also inside our little pot of gold were two military modified Remington 870 shotguns, and four M-9 Berettas. As we started to take the weapons off of their racks and into the control room, I noticed another rifle, semi-hidden in the rear of the locker, behind the ammo cans. Reaching back into the locker to see what it was, I noticed that my hand was about to pull a Russian weapon out of a U.S. missile silo weapons locker. If it were not for the inscription on the weapon, I would have forever wondered what it was doing there in the first place.

In English, and some Russian the following was written:

For Colonel James Butler, USAF
"Cold War 1945-1989"
Dimitre Nikolaevich

It didn't take much for me to have a decent guess at why this weapon was here. Although my Russian is rusty, and never was any good anyway, I still recognized "polkovnik" as Colonel. I knew also that "Voyna" meant war, and the cold war was considered officially over in 1989. This meant that "Khalodny" was probably Russian for cold. This Russian AK-47 was more than likely a gift of good will from one fallen superpower military man, to Colonel Butler. Of course I had no idea who Butler was, but it was probably a safe bet that he commanded this post sometime during the cold war and had encountered his Russian adversary prior to the fall of the USSR.

This made me wonder what Mr. Butler had sent comrade Nikolaevich in return. I guess I will never know the answer. This weapon looked in excellent shape. I decided to take it to my compartment as sort of a souvenir, a souvenir much more useful than a shot glass.

We are now well armed with at least one military grade weapon available per person. Unfortunately, the females have no idea how to operate any of these weapons, and this was something that needed to be fixed soon. John and I went out again to better hide the aircraft.

Now, you would have to be pretty much on top of it to find it. John is still busy figuring out all the various systems of this complex. There is still the intermittent mechanical sound coming from somewhere in the facility, and John and I are trying to isolate the source. After examining literally dozens of photos, we were unable to find any sign of our attacker(s) from the other night.

I half wondered if (he/she/they) would be good enough to locate us just by the general direction the aircraft was headed. I knew we would have been shot down that night if I had left the strobes and take off lights on. A well-lighted target would have been easy to hit. The gunman was just aiming at the sound of the engine.

We are all taking turns monitoring the cameras at regular intervals, and John seems to think there may be a motion sensing function that the cameras are able to utilize with the right commands. For the time being, we have some weapons to clean.

April 26th
1954 hrs

Took some time, but finally cleaned all the weapons that needed it. I wouldn't mind getting some ammunition for the AK-47, as it requires a different caliber than its domestic comrade, the M-16. I spent the day yesterday teaching Tara and Jan how to load, aim, and adjust for wind with the rifles. I feel that those skills are in high demand these days.

In a fit of boredom, John and I took some satellite photographs of Houston. We were unable to locate any survivors. At one point, we thought we had a decent lead, as on the roof of one of the taller buildings we saw a hastily made banner that read simply, "HELP." It wasn't until John increased the magnification that we discovered that "HELP" had already arrived in the form of the undead. There were four of them on the roof, milling about, probably the same ones that constructed the makeshift banner.

We have also been studying the diesel generator manuals for this complex. There are large batteries that we had not noticed before in the back of the generator room, out of plain sight. Upon closer inspection, the battery gauges were in the red, not the green. John and I researched the meaning of the gauge being in the red, and found out that it meant the batteries had lost charge from neglect. We practiced the start up sequence, and then performed the real thing. It wasn't until the noise was so loud that John and I had to shout at each other before we realized the implications of our actions. We rushed to the control room and John immediately switched to the camera at the main access doors.

They were still there, and they didn't seem to react to the noise. John and I were a small distance from the generator room here in the control room. It wasn't loud, but you could definitely hear the steady hum of an engine. Satisfied that we did not unleash hell upon ourselves, we headed back to the generator room to monitor the battery gauges. They were steadily moving toward the green. It was only two hours before they were at full charge, and we shut down the generators. Main power is still holding, miraculously.

In the back of my mind, I keep feeling the ripple effect of what that muzzle flash meant. Why would someone shoot at another human survivor, unless said survivor was trying to hurt them? I don't see what joy another human being would get out of killing a living person in a world like this. Since January, I had definitely done my share of killing however; I haven't had the choice of leveling my weapon on a living human. In light of recent events, this may certainly change.

Hotel 23 — Silo Doors

Amigos

April 29th

2305 hrs

It has been a very uneventful few days. I have been checking the security cameras at regular intervals for any sign of irregular undead movement. I feel that the ones at the front access door are not totally useless. They will tell me if anything living gets near them. I consider them sort of my back up front door alarm. Considering the threat of possible living human aggressors, we spent some time over the past couple of days checking our physical security. We made sure to lock the hatch to the silo so that no one can climb down like we did, and get in. Still no joy on closing the silo doors. John seems to think that some sort of failsafe was in place to ensure that no one aborted a launch by simply shutting the doors.

Bits and pieces of the old world keep flooding my mind. I am not sure the fate of the friends I once knew. Their names are all but forgotten. I do miss them. One friend owned his own company, and was a successful businessman. He had a wife and kids. We were close. Part of my mind wants Craig to still be alive surviving with his family, however the other part of me just wishes his death were swift, as I feel those that died quickly, were the lucky ones. My friend Mike was leaving for New York to attend a culinary arts school there.

Ironically, the bullet that killed him was released from Hotel 23. This facility was the backup for the rogue bombers. I suppose I would rather go in a hot flash, than be torn apart by the hands of over twelve million undead. Duncan was a professional lounger that didn't believe in working full time. I suppose he was the one that had it right. Instead of being a hamster on a wheel for his last days, he continued his mantra of just being Duncan.

April 30th

2010 hrs

Heard a loud "thud" coming from somewhere in the complex about an hour ago. After checking the inside of the complex, we could not find the source of the sound.

2342 hrs

I'm hearing strange thumping noises from inside the complex. John and I are headed to check the security cameras now.

Truth and Consequences

May 1st
1424 hrs

The loud thump that was heard last night kept playing back in my mind. The sound appeared to come from inside the complex, however after a good inside inspection we found nothing. This morning that changed. We started hearing intermittent tapping, bumping sounds, again coming from inside of the complex. We again checked the cameras just to make sure. We checked the perimeter. John sat there for a minute and suggested, "Why not check all of them just in case?" I agreed and we began flipping through the cameras inside the complex.

They all showed clear, until we reached the missile silo camera. The launch must have clouded up the lens, because it wasn't very clear at all. John tried to switch to night vision mode, but apparently this camera was not designed for that function.

We continued to watch. A large dark figure moved in front of the camera, blocking the view momentarily. Then more sounds coming from inside the complex. Whatever or whoever, was tapping, pounding on the silo walls. I decided to go topside and look down into the silo from above, avoiding the possibility of putting myself in a potentially compromising (deadly) position.

I grabbed my carbine and started climbing the steps of the alternate exit leading to the helicopter pad, and the large silo chasm. The cool May air rushed in as I opened the sealed door. I stepped out into the sunshine, allowing my eyes to adjust. The first thing that caught my eye was the gate. It wasn't closed. I walked up to the gate, and checked it for forced entry. Nothing seemed wrong, except that there was some dirt on the buttons themselves. For all I knew any of us could have pushed the buttons with dirty hands so I dismissed this and walked over to the gaping hole in the ground.

Fearing that the gusty wind could push me into the hole, I crouched down into a prone position and eased my head over the side. Looking down into the hole, I found the source of all the strange noise from the night before and this morning. At the bottom of the silo, stood a mangled Air Force officer with his arm showing numerous compound fractures sticking out from his rotted skin. The hideous creature took notice of the shadow I cast below and attempted to climb the ladder up to his meal.

I almost laughed at the creature as it attempted its ascent. I suppose the fall from up here broke its arm and dislocated its shoulder. It would put its foot up on the first rung and then fall backwards from lack of coordination.

This undead former officer was dressed in exactly the same uniform as the two that were here when we showed up. Coupled with this and the fact that something had to open the cipher lock, I assumed the worst. This could suggest that these creatures may retain more than primitive residual memories. This officer must have been stationed here and succumbed to his death months earlier, only to stumble here last night and somehow remember how to punch the five-digit code to get in.

Now came the task of disposal. I couldn't afford the full on noise of my weapon being fired from up here. So I decided to climb down into the silo half way to shoot it. This wasn't something I was wild about, but I would rather do it this way, than draw the attention of the legions at the front of the complex.

I swung my legs over the edge and began my descent, weapon slung over my shoulder. At half way down, I held on with my left hand, and readied my weapon. The creature was rabid, and wanted nothing more than me to fall down and break my legs. I would be helpless as it devoured me. Thinking of this creature's spite towards me, I took aim and destroyed it.

I told John the news, and he definitely showed concern about the gate, and how the creature was probably the thing that opened it. I wanted to check its pockets, but I was in no mood to do it now. We would leave it there until tomorrow before we took it topside for disposal.

May 4th

2109 hrs

My mother would have turned fifty today. All hope is lost at the prospect of my family's survival. John and I changed the code on the exterior gate in the event we had another visitor. The day after our encounter with the "hole jumper," John and I decided to check his pockets. Absolutely nothing. He did however have something that caught my eye. On his left arm was a nice new looking Omega wristwatch. No use letting it go to waste.

The hour hand of the watch was one hour behind mine, due to this thing being unable to set daylight savings time. Other than that, it was still running accurately. It was an automatic and the movement of the corpse kept it alive. It was a nice find.

I am going out to check the aircraft in the cover of darkness tonight. Played with Lara today. Took Annabelle for a walk also. I let them roam free while I repaired the weak barrier surrounding the launch doors. There was an open spot where the corpse tripped over it and fell.

The wind shifted and Annabelle could smell them. The hair on her back stood up like a hedgehog, and she started barking. I pointed at the dog, and signaled for Laura to pick her up. It was pretty funny seeing little Laura trying to hold Annabelle while she wiggled. Enough of their world for one day, I suppose. Back inside we went.

May 7th
2036 hrs

Although the sound of the evening rain cannot be heard from inside the complex, I know it is there, just like the moans of the dead outside. Thunder and lightening have dominated the sky for hours now. The CCT picture is crackling as the lightening bursts hit near the complex. I suppose no storm could be of harm to us under the ground, however, I bet a tornado could take down our perimeter fence.

In between interference, I can make out the undead horde outside. Many of them are being blown off their feet by the wind, or being knocked down by the ebbing tidal wave of the other undead. Digging through the lounge area yesterday, I found a book titled "Oryx and Crake," by Margaret Atwood. I spent most of the night last night, and most of the day today reading it. I suppose it sort of parallels my situation, in a weird sort of way. No need to go into it, I doubt anyone else will be reading it anyway. Sort of depressing I suppose. John and I have been hearing chatter on the HF radios. It is definitely not garbled, however it seems that the people/persons speaking are using some sort of brevity code. How optimistic of them to assume anyone gives a shit.

Tara and I worked out together this morning. Push-ups, sit-ups, side straddle hops..."We won't stop 'till our freakin' heart stops." That little line brings back memories of my Marine Corps drill instructor from officer candidate school. What a fucking hard ass. I bet the son of a bitch is still alive somewhere, making someone miserable at this very moment.

May 10th
1953 hrs

On the night of the 8th, something caused the undead at the front of the complex to move away for a few hours. Watching on the cameras outside the front complex, I could see their attention diverted. Their rotting heads swiveled around in that familiar expression of food for the taking. The hundreds in view of the camera faded into the night. What they were after, I do not know. William and I have a theory that it could be the same person or group of people that shot at me in the aircraft. It only makes sense that they would scout this area, considering its obvious value for sheltering.

More chatter on the HF band. I was able to make out the following words: Band, offensive, and perimeter. I am not certain the order they were spoken, or the context in which they were used, however they could mean many things. We have a few thousand rounds of ammunition from the weapons locker, but I don't think we could repel intruders if we were grossly outnumbered. If they breached the complex defenses, they could defeat us.

The girls have been learning how to aim the carbines, however I feel it necessary for them to get some actual live fire time with them to be at least semi proficient. It would be lunacy to do it anywhere near the complex, as it would only draw them to our position and they would see us flee back inside the fence. I will begin preparing for a daytime outing with Jan and Tara in order to make sure they can fire the assault rifles when the time comes.

I overheard Jan teaching Laura some basic mathematics. I suppose with no school around for her to attend, it is not a bad idea for Jan to keep Laura learning. Annabelle is getting fat from lack of exercise and lack of real dog food.

May 14th
2209 hrs

I took the girls on a little outing on the 11th. Hiked out about one mile around the complex so that we could see the main entry doors in the far distance. It was William, Jan, Tara, and myself. We took Jan and Tara out so that they could become more proficient with the M-16s that we had acquired from the weapons locker. Instead of wasting ammunition, we decided to aim for the undead at the complex for target practice. We eased inward toward the main entry area until we were about five hundred yards away, and within a clear field of vision.

I was spotting with binoculars while William kept a scan behind us. The Jan and Tara were already loaded and carried extra magazines. It was now time for them to actually get to fire the weapons. They pulled back the charging handles, and I heard the clicks as they released, shoved the round into the chamber. They took aim. I plugged my ears with 9mm rounds, and pulled up the binoculars as they fired. With nothing really to aim at, they fired at center mass in the crowd. Through the binoculars, I could see some of them fall, while others had brown dust blowing off of them in places where the rounds hit. They weren't the only ones here for target practice, it was MY turn.

William, Jan, Tara and I waited as the massive formation of the undead began moving toward the location of the gunshots and away from Hotel 23. The girls continued to pick off the stragglers as I loaded the M-203 mounted to the M-16 I was carrying. I had never fired a grenade through one of these before, but I had carefully read the manual over and over the past few days.

A group of at least three hundred was making their way toward our location, with a straggler here and there around the formation. There were more than this behind that group that finally got the picture something was happening and they too started our direction. The first group was about two hundred yards away when I fired the grenade. Not knowing the characteristics of the weapon, I over compensated and fired between the group of three hundred, and the larger group behind them. I killed some from both groups. The girls were still firing, aiming for headshots. William was still checking our flank, trusting us to be his forward eyes.

I slid the second round into the launcher. This time my aim put the grenade into the center of the nearest group. The round exploded, and fragged at least fifty of them. The concussion knocked half of them on their ass. It was like watching dominos fall on themselves. Sure enough, many of them slowly lumbered back onto their feet. Now that I knew the capabilities of this weapon, and the girls had some real world experience with the M-16, it was time to head back. We disappeared into the tree line and circled back, hidden by the foliage, we returned to the complex.

Trouble in Paradise

May 16th

1202 hrs

We are now under siege. This morning at around 0530 hours we heard a loud noise from above and within minutes started hearing those familiar thumping sounds, very similar to the sound heard when the lone undead Air Force officer fell into the open silo. I lost count of the thumps.

Must have been twenty, maybe thirty. John, Will and I went to the control room and reversed the surveillance recording to a spot on the hard drive just before the loud noise. On the screen we saw the source of the original noise. A tow truck, similar to the trucks that tow tractor-trailers, was chained to the cipher lock gate/chain link fence. I could tell the driver had put the hammer down due to the mud and grass they were throwing up behind the tires. The gate, and a ten foot section of fence instantly uprooted out of the ground leaving a fifteen foot open space in the fence. The tow truck was all but surrounded by undead as it sped off into the night. We could see them pouring into the perimeter, tripping over the destroyed fence section.

We switched back to normal monitoring mode, but it didn't do much good. I caught the last few seconds of seeing five men put potato sacks (or something like it) over the cameras. Why didn't they destroy the cameras? The only camera left is the main front access camera. I assume they either didn't see it, or the dense population of undead was too great in that section to deal with it. We hear intermittent sounds from topside, but really have no way of knowing what is being planned.

I theorize that if we were to open the silo access doors, we would have a small army of beaten and battered undead to contend with. I can hear the sounds of their muffled pounding even now. They want out of their cylindrical prison. That isn't entirely true. They really only want one thing.

Another thing that is on my mind was why didn't they just drive the huge tow truck right through the fence? It would have been safer than getting out and attaching a chain to both the fence and the truck. Unless... —They were trying to minimize damage to the compound. John is working the main camera. He can see vehicles moving behind the mass of undead. Just when they get into plain view, they turn off the beaten path toward the back of the complex where we are. John counted six vehicles in all, excluding the tow truck. The sun was just coming up. Right now, it is quiet. It is going to be a long day.

2018 hrs

I don't know why we didn't think of this before. They placed bags over the cameras to disable, not destroy them. John switched the camera view from normal to thermal. We were able to see any and all living human movement through the cloth bags as if they weren't even there. We have been panning the cameras back and forth, getting head counts on their numbers. Their orange and red glow can be seen swarming around numerous vehicles in their group. Multiple gunshots are apparent. As they fire, I can see the hot flash of their muzzles through the thermal cam. Their weapons don't look military. They look more like hunting rifles.

They keep moving, drawing the dead away from this area, then back again. I suppose they can't stay in one place due to the overwhelming number of undead in this area. They seem to be systematically herding them away, then back. Pretty ingenious. I suppose they have been surviving on the run since the beginning.

I bet they had been casing us for days, and they may have even been outside when we were testing our weapons. I don't hear any cutting tools or anything that would lead me to believe they were trying to force entry. The main camera in the front of the complex is still fully functional and shows an empty parking area on night vision mode.

These marauders have successfully cleared out our front door for us, but I have no idea if they are just waiting in the shadows to kill us at first opportunity. I placed my ear against the steel silo access door. I could hear them shuffling and moaning and beating the walls on the other side.

John's Deception

May 19th
1932 hrs

On the night of the seventeenth, they made their assault. We were watching on thermal cameras, and also on the unhindered front main camera when it happened. They brought crews of men to the launch bay pit where many undead had already fallen in. John's thermal cam had "whiteout" after a few minutes in the vicinity of the silo launch bay. After ten minutes went by, I used my gloved hand to feel the lower silo access door. The door was very thick and sturdy, but the heat from the fire on the other side was immense. They were burning out the undead in the pit. They wanted down below, and on the other side of the door I was standing at.

We had to formulate a plan. John told me that he saw on thermal, just before the whiteout occurred, four men carrying a large box toward the broken area of the chain link fence. It was probably some sort of cutting tool. Over the previous 24 hours (night of the sixteenth, to the seventeenth) I had observed them continuing to use the herding tactic to keep the undead manageable.

They had also brought a large eighteen-wheel gasoline tanker with their convoy. We saw this on the satellite image, before it became cloudy. I now estimated that their numbers to be fifty men, and nearly twenty vehicles.

We monitored the citizen's band radio for any intelligence. We could definitely hear them communicating. The code they were using sounded very familiar. Much like the brevity code we were hearing on the radio a couple of weeks ago. It might as well have been Chinese. It didn't matter at this point. Judging by the thermal whiteout, the fire was still raging. I had to think of a way to get topside without detection, and then somehow disorient them to the point of surrender. It was going to take all of us to pull this off.

Here was the plan; I instructed Jan to make a radio call to the marauders at a certain time. The call was to inform them that this was an official government base and that there are more than a hundred soldiers based here, all well armed. If they did not pull out, the soldiers would be authorized to use deadly force. She was instructed to make the call on the marauder's frequency exactly forty-five minutes after we left the compound.

John and I remembered back to when we first came to Hotel 23. We slept in a small, enclosed chain link fenced area with a large manhole lid on the inside. In our days since the discovery of this place, John, Will and I found out that it was, in fact an escape scuttle, designed as a redundancy exit if the others were knocked out. It was quite a ways from the silo doors and main entrance and chances are it went unnoticed.

The girls armed themselves with the carbines, and the shotguns. I instructed them on the proper use of the shotgun in a steel living area. If they aimed the shotgun down at the floor at approximately 45 degrees, the twelve gauge pellets would ricochet and destroy anything in front of them in the steel passage. I was taught this tactic in anti-terrorism training designed to repel terrorist boarders from U.S. naval vessels. They didn't even have to see their target when using this tactic.

I grabbed the M-16 with the M-203 launcher, all the ammo I would need, a blanket and my NVGs. John and William took M-16s and two M-9 pistols, and the binoculars. We headed for the emergency exit, approximately 1/3 of a mile down a dark access tunnel.

Some of the bulbs were burned out down here, and I constantly had to switch to night vision to lead John and Will to the hatch. John's hand stayed on my shoulder as I led them through the darkness. I could smell the fear in the air. We were all afraid. No one wanted to kill another human being, but this was our survival at stake.

We could take no chances with those that wished us harm. We were at the hatch. Jan would be starting her watch countdown now. I checked the time. It was 2155 hours. At 2240 she would be making her radio call. We couldn't risk using the hydraulic motor to open the heavy hatch. Everything in this place had a backup it seemed. We cranked the hatch open exactly two feet with sixty-two revolutions of the manual crank handle. There was no moon and it was cloudy out that night. I could see the distant glow of the silo fire just over the hill near from the fence we were in.

Together we climbed over the razor wire fence, using the blanket I had brought from the complex. We were on the other side. There was no undead movement to either side of us at this side of the fence. We low crawled up the embankment to level our vantage point with the bandits. There they were. Using the binoculars, I started a head count on them. I counted forty-five in all. Many of the vehicles they were driving looked rather expensive. Many had Landrovers and full sized Hummers. They were all gathered around the fence near their vehicles and the large fuel truck used to re-supply them with dead dinosaurs.

At this point I was at a loss. We were grossly outnumbered and would easily lose in a firefight. All we could do was wait for Jan's radio message and hope they would pull out. It was 2215... I could hear them talking faintly. I switched back on my NVGs to check the darker areas outside the burn of the silo fire. Funny, I could see the bags illuminated by the infrared beam of the camera inside them. The bags on the cameras looked like a green version of those old propane camp lights that used the cloth back and propane to generate light.

It was 2235. Minutes seemed like hours. In five minutes we would know what we were up against. The marauders were dressed in a mixture of blue jeans, and camouflage pants. Many of them looked fat and out of shape, their guts hanging over their pant line. It didn't matter, you don't have to be skinny to pull a trigger and hit your target.

Go time, 2240. I checked my watch and nodded to John and Will to remain very quiet. Nothing. No sign that they heard Jan's call. Then it came. I heard the group make the sound "Shhhh!" all in unison, signaling their fellow bandits to be quiet. Then...loud laughter from the group and one person shouting, "FUCK YOU BITCH! YOU HAVE IT, WE WANT IT!" Then came loud laughter, cursing and weapon's fire into the night sky.

I had to grab William's arm to keep him from standing up in anger. The flames were disappearing, and I could no longer see the tops of them as they sunk below the lip to the silo doors. Time was running out. Using the binoculars, I could see some sort of welding/cutting device being lugged inside the fence. These men wanted us dead.

It was a matter of survival of the fittest. I made the decision. Rather than wait for them to overpower us inside the complex, I decided to hit them while they were all close together. It is a decision that will haunt me forever. I told John and Will to get down as I loaded the M-16 mounted grenade launcher. I knew how far I was from the tanker. I adjusted the sights for my one hundred meter target. I sat there meditating for a moment, pondering on my decision. No more time to think. No more time to hesitate...I pulled the trigger.

The grenade whistled through the air toward the fuel tanker. It landed about two or three meters from the middle of the trailer and detonated, sending hundreds of steel shards into the metal skin holding the thousands of gallons of gasoline. Then came a huge explosion. I don't remember what happened after that.

My next memory was of John and William taking turns giving me CPR at the base of the razor wire fence. I later found out that the concussion of the blast knocked me off my feet and threw me backwards ten meters into the bottom section of the fence. They noted that I was lucky to hit a center section of the fence, and not the post, or the razor wire.

I have been in bed since that day, recovering from burns and a probable concussion, according to Jan. John and William carried me back to the command center and made the radio call out to the rest of the marauders. We assumed that some were out on "herding" duty. John broadcasted the following message on all available frequencies:

"For the rogue group that has recently carried out
hostilities against the government launch facility:
Be advised that four Apache helicopters were dispatched
to this area to neutralize all hostile forces in the vicinity.
Any further hostilities will result in
maximum retaliation to your faction."

John repeated this message for half an hour. As of right now, we have received no response to the warning. I only hope John's deception worked. We may have won the battle for Hotel 23 but if a similar force decided to attack right now, we would fall. Either way you look at it, after killing almost fifty living men, I have some serious issues to deal with. In a way I was happy to be knocked out to the point of near death, if only because I could not hear their last screams.

Afterword

Thank you for traveling with me into the world of the undead and I hope that you enjoyed reading *Day by Day Armageddon* as much as I enjoyed writing it. This is not the end of the story and rest assured that you will hear more from our survivor at Hotel 23. Although the Global War on Terrorism has taken up much of my time, I still find time to delve into the mind of the man on the run, trapped in a dead world. I owe the character and the fans of this novel that much.

There will be a sequel.

—Keep your doors locked,

JL Bourne

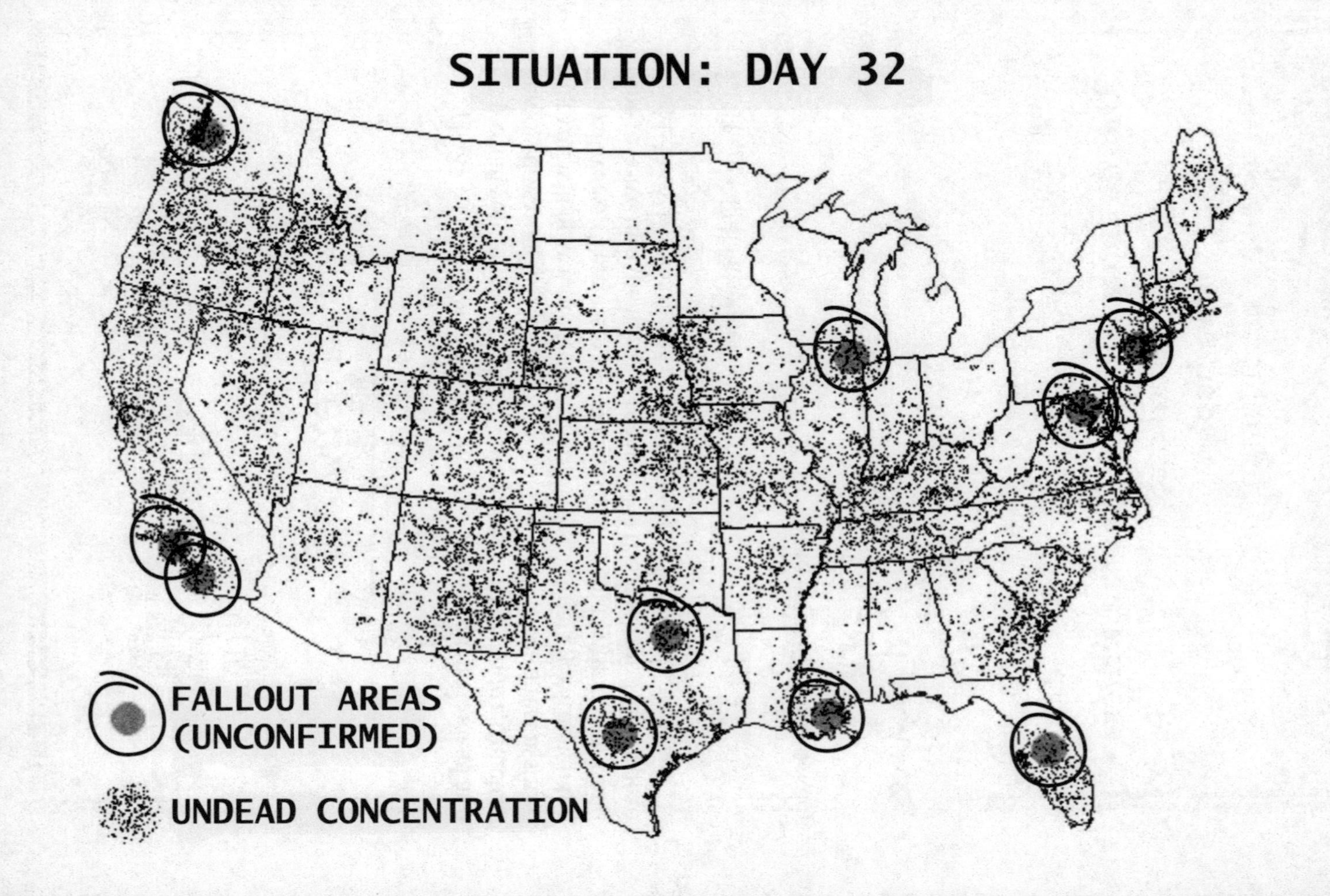
SITUATION: DAY 32
FALLOUT AREAS
(UNCONFIRMED)
UNDEAD CONCENTRATION
X:/NORAD/SCI/TALENT_KEYHOLE/fallout/UNDEAD

DEREK GUNN

THE ESTUARY

Excavations for a new shopping centre in the town of Whiteshead have unearthed a mysterious contagion that threatens the lives of the townspeople. Now the residents are trapped within a quarantine zone with the military on one side and ravenous hordes of living dead on the other. Escape is no longer an option.

Far out in the mouth of the estuary sits a small keep. This refuge has always been unassailable, a place of myth and legend. Now it's the survivors' only hope of sanctuary. But there are thousands of flesh-eating infected between them and the keep, and time is running out...

ISBN: 978-1934861240

Five novels of the living dead by zombie fiction master Eric S. Brown: *Season of Rot*, *The Queen*, *The Wave*, *Dead West*, and *Rats*.

"A VERITABLE GRAB-BAG OF ZOMBIE GOODNESS. A LITTLE OF THIS, AND A LITTLE OF THAT, A LOT OF BRAINS..."
—Z.A. Recht,
author of *Plague of the Dead*

ISBN: 978-1934861226

More details, excerpts, and purchase information at

www.permutedpress.com